D1627739

This book should be returned to any branch of the
Lancashire County Library on or before the date shown

	1 9 SEP 2008
2 3 MAY 2007	1 4 OCT 2008
- 2 JUN 2007	1 6 FEB 2009
2 6 JUL 2007	
	- 1 AUG 2009
- 2 AUG 2007	8/2/10
2 4 AUG 2007	2 0 DEC 2010
- 7 DEC 2007	
1 9 APR 2008	
- 9 JUL 2008	
2 6 JUL 2008	

Under the Dust

Jordi Coca was born in Barcelona in 1947. He was first drawn to writing at the age of fourteen, an experience he has described, not without irony, as an 'enlightenment'. He has become a leading figure in Catalan culture and literature, working in the fields of narrative fiction, drama, poetry, criticism and translation. He is also a teacher of drama, being head of the Barcelona Theatre Institute from 1988 to 1992, and is a theatre director and playwright.

From his first novel *Els Lluïsos* (republished as *Un d'Aquells Estius* 'One of Those Summers') in 1971, he has published over thirty works, including translations of the Japanese poet Matsuo Basho and Belgian Nobel Prize winner Maurice Maeterlinck, stage adaptations of Ibsen, Maragall and Sophocles, as well as numerous novels including *La Japonesa* ('The Japanese Woman'), *Dies Meravelloses* ('Wonderful Days') and *Lenu*.

He has won numerous literary prizes, from the *Serra d'Or* for young writers in 1972 to the *Joanot Martorell de Gandia* in 2004 for his most recent novel *Cara d'Àngel* ('Angel Face'). *Under the Dust* (*Sota la Pols*) won the prestigious *Premi Sant Jordi* in 2000.

Jordi Coca has been actively involved in Catalan politics over many years and is a regular contributor to Catalan newspapers and television. He lives in Barcelona.

Richard Thomson was born in London but has lived much of his adult life outside Britain, mainly in Catalunya where he moved in 1986, learning Catalan from friends and television commentary of FC Barcelona matches. He is now a translator and editor and currently lives on a farm in Wales with Sarah and their dogs.

Under the Dust

Jordi Coca

PARTHIAN

Parthian
The Old Surgery
Napier Street
Cardigan
SA43 1ED
www.parthianbooks.co.uk

First published in Catalan as Sota la pols
© Jordi Coca 2001
All Rights Reserved
In association with Pontas Literary & Film Agency

This edition first published in English by Parthian 2007
Translation © Richard Thomson 2007

Translated with the support of the Ramon Llull Institute

LLLL institut
ramon llull

ISBN 978-1-905762-39-2

Cover design by Lucy Llewellyn
Inner design by books@lloydrobson.com
Printed and bound by Dinefwr Press, Llandybïe, Wales

Published with the financial support of the Welsh Books
Council.

British Library Cataloguing in Publication Data

A cataloguing record for this book is available from the British
Library.

For my brothers and sister

Je me souviens
Des jours anciens
Et je pleure

Paul Verlaine

Like an Angel

When I look at the old photographs from my childhood, my heart sinks. I don't look sickly, but I'm thin, with big sad eyes and untidy hair. In the same pictures there are other kids laughing and playing, while I always seem subdued and lifeless.

I've forgotten many of those children who, in one of the most dreadful pictures, are lined up around the teacher in the school playground. Most are twelve or thirteen, us younger ones in front, all of us wearing striped smocks and scarves tied around our necks, surrounding the tall thin ascetic man whose job it was to teach us reading, writing, arithmetic, 'National Spirit Training' and not much else.

I've also still got a portrait of my brother, who died back then in 1947, a few months after he was born. He was fair and beautiful like an angel. He was born at the end of January, and fell ill in the summer. Fever consumed him and meningitis left him blind. I was eleven, and I remember my father going up onto the roof one night and spending hours emptying out buckets of water that first had to be collected from the fountain, in a desperate attempt to cool the house down. But his heroism was useless, because nothing could loosen the grip of the stifling, deadly heat that had taken over the house, nothing at all.

I never knew my maternal grandparents, who were from Menorca, but from the photographs I know grandfather was slim and wore rimless glasses. I've always thought that he looked rather like Pavese, whereas my grandmother, who died very young, appears in the pictures as a laughing girl in a pale dress. Of my other grandmother, Francesca, I remember her iron hands gripping me under my arms to lift me off the ground. There's also Grandfather Diego, with his shaved head and wide, crazed eyes, although really I should not remember him because he was shot at the castle on Montjuïc at the end of the war. In the family, our talks about grandfather's misadventures always ended up in screaming rows. It appears he was short and nervous and often used to come home after a week without a word from him, drunk, dirty, defeated and ridden with lice. My grandmother would get hold of him then and take him to his bed like a little child. In one or two photographs there is a fat, dark-skinned woman, gypsy-like, with her hair tied back, looking out with an insolent air. I don't know who she is.

A little later my grandmother died, ill and embittered by what had happened, and then the wretched misfortune of my brother befell us. My sad look in the photographs must be because of all this, but I also remember the shame I felt at having to wash naked in the yard in the summertime, and the irritation of going to the barber's. I would struggle up into the mechanical chair, terrified, and then after a moment my father would decree, 'Short'.

I immediately felt the hand clippers go up the back of my neck as they sheared my hair, sending a horrible tickling all over me as they went over my skull. Then I felt the shiver down my back, descending through my legs and stopping at my feet, which I couldn't help but wiggle. The young barber's thin, long, cruel fingers, very white and cold, made all this extremely unpleasant... But it was even worse if I got the old one, who didn't talk and turned my head with one hand, like a machine, first to one side, then the other.

Everything in that barber's was distressing: the amount of hair on the floor, the way they had of hiding it behind the door, how they shook out the gown, full of little cigarette burns; the overpowering smell of hair lotion, the soap dishes full of the white paste they mixed with water to shave the customers, the ashtrays overflowing with yellow butts, the sky blue colour of the walls... Poverty appalled me. I didn't know anything else, but I loathed old things, broken furniture and worn out clothes. In bed I would say to myself that I had been born into a dead world, full of dead things. The barbers were dead, the mirrors were dead, the damp walls of the house were dead, the basin I had to wash my face in was dead, the desks at school were dead, the food I ate was the food of the dead, the cutlery was the cutlery of the dead, the sheets were cold stained shrouds... And these things caused me infinite disgust, which I had to hide.

'My brother's in heaven,' I used to say to my schoolmates, and one day Ramon, a fair, green-eyed boy, bigger than me, replied that according to his mother our family had been punished for the business with my grandfather. We were all

3

guilty, he said and there's no way guilty people can go to heaven. I always studied people's eyes, and Ramon's eyes were malevolent, watching out for my reaction.

The school smelled unbearably of chalk, damp and disinfectant, and we were so cold in the middle of winter neither we nor the teachers could take off our overcoats. It was a brick-built building on a corner, and looked like a soulless fortress, full of dark windows. You went in through a huge entrance that led to the hall, where there were two staircases. A dingy one descended to the cement playground surrounded by barren chestnut trees; a wider one went up to the floors above. The hall, stairs and corridors were lifeless, but I remember the classrooms being full of light, with very high ceilings.

In the mornings we went straight down to the playground and quickly lined up, many of us in short trousers. With our arm raised, feeling the tightness of our coats, we sang 'Cara al Sol', the Fascist National Anthem. As the grandson of the one who was shot, I felt all the others watching me out of the corner of their eyes. Later, in the classroom, the teacher indicated with his pointer names written on the blackboard from the day before, asking questions that I had trouble understanding. Because I knew he never asked me anything, I spent my time watching my classmates. One was thin and scared-looking, another was lame and hopped along when he ran, the one with the glasses always seemed to have a snotty nose, the tallest one kept an eye on us.... In a perverse way I felt drawn to Ramon who was older, the one with the green eyes who said there was no way my brother could be in heaven.

Perhaps it was because of all this that in the summer, when we went out at night to cool down, I would sit with the

4

adults. I remember a white-haired lady with a lined face and small brown distant eyes who lived on our street. Her husband had gone off to the front as a volunteer and she never saw him again. I also recall a bright, happy-eyed girl from Andalucía who had just got married, and a fat woman with a coal-black look in her eye. Her tall grey-haired husband worked as a nightwatchman at a factory down the street and sometimes came to sit with us. He would put my cap on my head and say, 'Right, off you go and play...'

I hated that cap and took it off immediately but the truth is that I looked forward to seeing the watchman because he was the only one who noticed I was sitting with the grown-ups. I didn't like playing. Playing meant going with a group of lads round the back of the white-walled clinic, and clambering over the garden wall in the dark. It meant scrabbling across the gravel and somehow climbing up to a window from where I was told you could see the nurses undressing and changing into their uniforms. I'd never seen a thing, and besides, I was scared of hurting myself and got quickly tired of it. Or perhaps they would decide to go off to a derelict house, find a way in and start smoking. Or go up the streets that led to the mountain spring and piss on the little pipe where the water trickled out.

Sometimes, instead of going out to cool down, uncles, aunts and cousins came to our house for supper. An old square table appeared in the yard, around which my father and uncle often argued. My cousins played with picture cards, while my mother and her sister stood in the kitchen twittering away until someone made them come out. I liked hearing my mother and Aunt Neli speak Menorcan, which they only did when they were together. And I thought it was funny that because my aunt had married one of my father's brothers,

5

Uncle Pere, who was easy-going and a bit of a joker, my cousins and I had the same surname. One of them, Esther, was older, and the other, Lola, was about the same age as me. Afterwards, when everyone had gone home and I was in bed, the walls shrank, creaked, and in a language only I understood, they talked about inexplicable things, things I forgot about straightaway, but whose bitter aftertaste was still present when I opened my eyes again.

After my brother's death, my father, in his own way, became very affectionate to my mother and me. Very early in the mornings, when he was going off to work, he made us get up and showered us with kisses as we went with him to the front door. I watched him jump on his bicycle and turn to wave us goodbye as he began to pedal away. I thought I would never see him again, and I went back to bed with a lump in my throat, unable to erase the harrowing image of a man on a bicycle in an empty street, a man on whom all manner of misfortune fell. Later I heard my mother doing her chores in the kitchen and I lay still, with the covers up around my nose, listening to the walls and not understanding why I had to go to school in a few hours. What the teachers said meant nothing, the local lads had their own concerns and took no notice of me, what was happening to us was unbelievably cruel and yet all the same the day dawned slowly.

A winter of torrential rain, wind and cold arrived; my father, his eyes light and intense, decided to fix the leaks in the roof. Because he did it too quickly, without preparing his materials or the tools he needed, he kept having to come down off the roof sodding the whole bloody thing. When he went up the ladder he looked like a giant to me. After a while I heard him curse because the cement had dried on him too quickly. I pictured him in terrible battle with invisible, powerful forces until, finally, he ended up smashing the solid washbasin in the yard, buggering and fucking everything and everyone a thousand times over. I watched him with both admiration and fear because these domestic repairs, at which he was quite useless, always culminated in a truly awesome finale which to me was fascinating and terrifying at the same time. My father's clumsiness, the tools he didn't know how to use, the bags of cement that burst in his hands, were always the overture to an outbreak of wild inexplicable violence. When these things happened, my mother and I knew that at any moment the curses, kicks, swearing and hateful looks would ensue.

Generally speaking, the episode would end with him going off to find someone to help, and once the work had been finished, a tortuous, labyrinthine search for the guilty parties began. My mother made herself as scarce as possible, feigned ignorance, changed the subject.... Meanwhile I got out of the house. It was all useless though, because my father's inability to plug a leak had to be personified in a culprit who received unwarranted accusations and threats. We then had the contemptuous, brutal insults, a blazing shouting match, the shoves, then the slam of the door that meant he was off to the bar for hours. When he came back in the middle of the night, he always made me stand on my bed, bear-hugged me till it hurt. Fixing his stare on me with those transparent eyes he had, he asked me if I loved him. Shivering from the cold, I didn't know how to reply, and moved my head vaguely. After a while, lying in my bed I heard my mother and father talking. I couldn't make out what they were saying, but I'm sure that it was during these conversations that they thought of sending me to Menorca. My mother said that she'd put up with the war, with what had come afterwards, that she had put up with everything, until the situation had become impossible and that I had to go away. I'm not sure, but I do remember her, at another time, running her hand through my hair and saying, 'You'll be all right there...'

I only knew the people from the island from the sepia-tinted photographs all around the house. We called them the aunts in Maó, but in fact Tonia and Roser were distant cousins of my maternal grandmother. Their names had quite a ring to them. There was one photograph of the two when they were young. Roser sat in a grand chair with Tonia standing by her side, one thin hand gripping the backrest. There was a hint of madness to them which always captivated me, or maybe it was just that the studio portrait didn't do them justice, making them look stiff.

Now it's clear that what was worrying me was not the reason for this separation but my inability to find answers to questions that were worrying me. Where would I sleep? Who would take me to the barber's? How long would I be away from home? What were the other people in Menorca like? I couldn't imagine leaving the single storey house where we lived, the yard that opened on to the street, my schoolmates... None of this was in itself pleasant, but knowing they were sending me away from it all made me feel completely unsettled. It was then that I latched on to Ramon and the boys in the gang. Ramon's fingernails were always dirty, but he was always followed around by four or five lads I remember very well. One was Perico, the lame one, another was called Joanet, very slim and small with too much brilliantine in his hair; there was also Antonio, who spoke half in Spanish and half in Catalan, then Salvador whose father was a chauffeur, Miquel who was very holy, and Jaume...

I saw them from time to time and played with them, but one day, not knowing why, I joined in with them and we went up Escornalbou Street. When we first arrived at the swimming pool gardens we walked around, doing nothing much, our hands in our pockets because of the cold. It was very quiet and the water in the pool was green and soupy. We sat down on one side, from where we could see the little hut at the far end, and I could feel my lips were numb and my nose frozen and red. There was a big Falangist flag, and on the platform in front of it some young lads in blue shirts and crossbelts were smoking. After a while a bugle sounded and the young uniformed men quickly threw away their cigarettes and lined up. A white-haired man gave the order to fall in and said, in Spanish, 'Close ranks!'

The boys stuck out their arms so their fingers touched the shoulder of the lad in front, and there was an enthralling silence.

'Attention!'

They all stood to attention at once, in one single movement, and remained completely still, looking up. For a few minutes we were captivated by them and the clear orders that rang out under the blue sky.

'Right turn!'

Antonio was drooling with envy. Joanet was scared and watched Ramon out of the corner of his eye. Perico was holding his leg, which always gave him a bit of trouble. I was fascinated. Once or twice, going out with my parents on a Sunday, we had gone up to the swimming pool gardens, but that bore no relation to the immense peace and feeling of freedom that I experienced that morning.

'Left turn!'

They all turned like a machine to the left, facing us again, side by side, stock still. Then the white-haired man in charge inspected them, examining everyone from top to bottom. There was a slight movement in the air which made the silence still more intense and even prevented us from being able to speak. After a moment another loud, long order sounded: 'Fall... out!'

The parade broke up, and a happy buzz washed over us. Ramon said that if we went down there they would offer us a smoke, and we did gradually approach the young Falangists, but they only gave cigarettes to Ramon, Perico and Jaume, who were the oldest. Joanet and I watched them.

I knew by sight some of the lads who had done the drill. They didn't live in our street, but they went to the same school as us. I didn't know why, but I felt respect for them. Perhaps it was because I had heard my father and uncle arguing about the blue-shirted people at home. My father said that my grandfather had been shot by the Falangists, while my uncle said it had been the army people and that the blues had had nothing to do with it.

'But they're the same thing...' said my father.

'They're not the same...' pointed out my uncle, to which my father replied disdainfully, 'I'm going to get really pissed off with you in a minute...'

That day I thought they were harmless enough. They talked to us for a while, and as well as the tobacco they gave us a piece of bread with sausage on it, and a glass of fizzy lemonade that went up our noses.

Leaving the gardens we continued up the streets that went up towards the mountain. We walked slowly, at Perico's pace, saying nothing. I think all six of us felt the aftertaste of the military exercises we had witnessed. Arriving at the fountain, Joanet said he needed a shit and went and hid behind the bushes. Antonio peed against a tree. Perico was complaining about his leg and wishing he'd never been born. Ramon said nothing. He'd saved a yellow-papered cigarette in his pocket and took it out from time to time and sniffed it. I was tired, but I didn't want to go home because I thought, for no good reason at all, that Ramon could stop them sending me off to the island, and so it was better for me to be with him. But I still hadn't found the right moment to tell him what they wanted to do with me, and so I looked at him: those striking green eyes of his, and his special way of smiling while still being serious. When Joanet came back, pale, with his eyes shining, I heard him say 'What a relief...'

We turned up some steps that led to very steep streets with low houses, like ours but different, and slowly we went back down the hill. I had never been so far away from home on my own, and I was a bit elated following the boys through street after street. And then, to top it all off, Perico suggested taking me to see the dead people in the hospital.

'That way he'll know what's coming to him...' he said, referring to me.

I didn't know whether they were really going to take me there or if they were just joking, but as we got closer and closer to the hospital, everyone stopped talking. Even Antonio started getting cold feet, muttering he was tired and that he had seen it all before... But after a while, when we entered the grounds, he, as well as Ramon, Perico and Jaume, started walking furtively up and down to see if there was anybody around watching us. They told Joanet and me to keep our eyes peeled too and they took us through this place which seemed more like a village than a hospital, because there were separate buildings, divided by avenues and sad, dusty gardens.

'The people with tuberculosis are here,' said Joanet. 'Down there is where the rich women go to have babies. That building over there is where they take you if you've had an accident...'

After a good long time walking around looking out of the corner of our eyes at the men in white coats, we gathered again near the back entrance where we had come in.

'It's all right,' said Joanet to Ramon. 'No one's watching us,' and Ramon nodded. I didn't know where they were taking me but I was sure I wasn't going to see anything nice, and I told them I didn't want to go in.

'Stop pissing us about...' said Perico, seizing me by the arm and dragging me to hide behind an old building that seemed like the doorway to hell.

I don't know how long we were there, still, silent, sweating with the cold. To me it seemed like forever. My toes froze and I had goosebumps all over me. Perico grabbed my arm. From time to time Antonio looked up to check there were no white coats around. Finally they gave me a shove and we ran, right up against the wall, until we got to a door which Ramon opened very slowly with his foot. And we went in.

The first impression was that it was dark inside. There was only a white light coming down from high windows, a light that fell on three open coffins, inside which I saw two men and a woman, naked. It was fascinating, but I suddenly felt the cold freeze my bones and I sensed my legs about to give way. The dead people looked like little wax children, and the woman, the first naked woman I had ever seen, had lots of hair between her legs. One of the men was old, small and thin. The other had his hand on his belly. Then I felt Perico let go of my arm and the five of us all ran out towards the gardens. My heart was beating as if it had gone mad and when we stopped, I realised I had wet my trousers. Ramon laughed at me and said I was too much of a coward to hang out with them. But we were all agitated and immediately moved away from the hospital. Joanet was white as a sheet, his lips colourless, but he played the hard man, walking next to Antonio, who said nothing. Perico was limping more than ever and I could not get out of my mind those motionless bodies in the boxes. I didn't know what their faces were like, I had just seen them naked, in boxes, in the light that came in through the windows.

After a while Joanet and I said we were going home. The others went off down Independence Street and before they went out of sight gave us the short arm salute.

'They're animals...' Joanet said to me.

My head was all in a mess. I had entered a den of repulsion, and had shuddered at the sight of that dead woman, yet I had the satisfaction that for the first time I had acted almost like them, like one of the big boys. Joanet did not understand that to be big meant going through experiences like that, being brave. If they were going to take me off to my relations on that unknown island I'd better be tough. I still hadn't had a chance to talk to Ramon, but taking part in these adventures somehow brought me closer to him, and soon he would stop seeing me as the local coward. He, and Perico too, were always looking me in the eye and saying that to me, while Jaume laughed, 'You're a coward...'

That day, after seeing the dead people, I felt dirty and needed to wash. I told Joanet and he invited me over to his house because his mother wasn't in. When we got to the flat we took all our clothes off in the kitchen and washed with soap and water from top to toe.

'I'm tired,' said Joanet, as we dried ourselves off. I didn't reply, but after a while, as I was combing my hair, I asked if he wanted to come to our house for lunch. In a very low voice he said: 'If we snuff it, you know where we'll end up.' Joanet was more fixated than me by what we had seen, and later, as we walked slowly, I asked him what he would do if his parents wanted to leave him alone on an island.

'God...' he said, 'I'd shit myself.'

We ate very quickly so we could go back out again. The truth was that I had invited him over because I was embarrassed to be alone with my mother after seeing that naked woman. Everything was confused, everything was complicated and at least I could talk to Joanet. He didn't have Perico's bad temper, nor the serious character of Antonio, who was about to leave school to go and work as an assistant in an ironmonger's, but neither was he Ramon, who sometimes helped his parents in their grain shop. We dropped into the bar with the table-football, then went to the sunflower seed stall, and later on reached the fountain on the corner. There was no one there; it seemed as if the earth had swallowed up all the other kids. Joanet and I started playing marbles, not knowing what else to do.

He always said that his father had got qualified recently and worked in a factory where they made radios. He didn't earn much but couldn't complain, seeing as he had fought on the side of the reds, been in prison and had then had to do military service for ages... His elder brother was a mechanic, and instead of giving his pay to his mother spent it all on whores and tobacco. They were always rowing about this at his house, and he was afraid that when it was his turn to learn a trade, they would be really hard on him. His mother kept telling him 'There's no way I'm going to let the same thing happen with you, I can promise you that...' adding that at a bad time she had married a spineless weakling, and soon would have to go on the game in order to eat... Joanet was terrified of her and apparently, at night, imagined her as a man with a huge cock between her legs.

'I'd rather be an only child, like you...' he said to me that afternoon, without any malice. Although I didn't reply I didn't think it was right to talk about my brother's death like that.

A little later Riteta came down in a clean dress. She looked a bit of a pudding, sitting on the bench outside her house, but Antonio said you could start to see her breasts and that sometimes she opened her legs slightly to show him her knickers. She said nothing to us though, and because we were getting bored we left.

When we got to Pere's Bar, we saw Ramon playing table-football with an older lad who had his hair in a parting. Neither Joanet nor I knew who he was. We went up to them without saying anything and they made out they didn't even see us. When Ramon played with one of us, he used to pass the ball from one player to another, sort of dragging it forward, and almost without you realising it, he drilled it into the goal with a fierce drive. He knew a lot about table-football, but that day it was more difficult for him because the other lad, as soon as he got the ball, fired it hard against the side and got it back with his forwards. Then Ramon, concentrating hard, got the defence and the goalkeeper in place so it looked as if no one could

15

score, but the other boy simply slotted the ball into the back of the goal opening. I'd always liked that sound of the heavy object rolling around in the wooden innards of the machine.

'What do you want?' said Ramon after a while, more surly than usual, because he was losing.

'Nothing,' replied Joanet, 'It's cold outside...'

'This is Ricardo,' said Ramon.

Later on four men came in rubbing their hands and sat themselves down to play dominoes. I liked hearing the unusual words and expressions they used as they tapped the pieces on the marble and placed them at one of the ends:

'Whistle.'

'Two doubles.'

'Can't you count or what?'

Pere's wife, who was white-haired and fat, brought them little glasses of wine. From what I'd heard at home, one of the sons of Pere and this woman had died at the front. I didn't remember him, but apparently he was a good-hearted lad who more or less ran the business on his own. Back then, Pere didn't do much more than chat with the customers while his wife sewed. After the war, the two of them had to go back to running the bar, but the atmosphere wasn't the same and there weren't as many customers. We went there because of the football machines, and because there were lots of photographs of boxers on the walls.

'Adults always talk about the war,' remarked Joanet as we sat down at one of the marble tables in the back. 'All I can remember is sometimes I had a stomach-ache because my mother sent me to bed without any supper.'

'I don't remember anything,' I replied.

'Not even your grandfather?' he asked.

'No.'

'Is it true they shot him?'

'I suppose so.'

'What had he done?'

'I don't know.'

'The war was a pile of shit,' added Joanet a little later. 'I've heard people say sometimes they used to find men in the streets with a bullet in the head, or beaten to death, and that a lot of people have had to leave the country...'

'What do they live on, the people who've left?' I asked, because I was always interested in what people lived on.

'Don't know,' he replied. 'No idea.'

My mother was always warning me not to talk to anyone about this sort of thing, and kept saying they'd killed my grandfather because he was an idiot who talked too much, and that we had to be careful. Really, I didn't know what it meant to kill someone, to just kill them, just like that... Sometimes, when my father lost control, his eyes got all fired up and he started shouting that they'd killed his father, asking us if he hadn't suffered enough, as if it was our fault. What would I think, he asked, if they told me they were going to kill me, and then he told me I could never kill anyone, I'd be completely incapable of it. And I went blank, as if my brain had been emptied, with nothing to say. Death was a horrible thing, I had seen that, and I didn't want to think about it, but for one reason or another it was always there: my grandfather, my grandmother, my brother, Mr Pere's son, those people in the hospital...

The days passed and at home no one said anything about me going off to Menorca. Maybe I had got confused and the journey had never been discussed. Either way I was obsessed by the idea of having to go and live with people I didn't know, to an island I didn't know either; I didn't even know if it was big or small. When I wasn't at school or out in the street so as to be around Ramon, I lay on my bed looking at those old photographs. The people from the island were odd, they seemed like beings from another world, ancient, as if stuck in a bygone age. They had an icy smile on their lips, or they looked at me so seriously that you could see they were putting on a pose for the picture. My father, slim, in overalls, me holding my cousin Lola's hand, the boy in my mother's arms...

Once we went to see my father at the warehouse where he worked, and he seemed strange to me. He looked more quiet, less nervy than he was at home. He introduced my mother to the supervisor, a tall man drenched in sweat, who put a hand on my face saying, 'Don't keep him long, lady...' She said she wouldn't and gave my father his lunchbox with his supper in it, because he was going to spend all night unloading trucks full of cloth that they chopped up in a machine and turned back into thread... That day my father's hair was full of dust and he seemed tired, and as soon as he'd given my mother a kiss on the cheek, he went to the truck and hauled an enormous sack onto his back. I was surprised to see he was wearing a black corset wrapped around his kidneys, and I thought it was funny how, with this sack on his back, he sort of ran with it into the warehouse instead of walking. At home I'd heard some pretty strong things said about the supervisor, that he was a son of a bitch, that he pocketed half the stuff that came into the warehouse, that he'd been one of the first of Franco's army to enter Barcelona...

'One of these days,' my father added more than once, 'I'm going to put his eyes out, slice him open and shit on his guts...'

One night my parents and I went back to the Versailles cinema, where they put on films and variety shows. It was the first time we'd been since the boy's death. I was fascinated by the moment after the film when the lights came up and, with a mechanical suggestive rumble, the great red curtain drew across in a big semi-circle, hiding the screen. The cinema turned into a theatre, and I enjoyed the thought that behind the curtain the singers, conjurers, comedians and illusionists were getting ready...

While the men went out for a smoke, the musicians checked their instruments. It was a magic moment because amid the notes of a piano and the odd sound of a trumpet, the women popped open the lemonade bottles and unwrapped the supper. When my father got back he sat down in his seat and took the omelette sandwich. He was in a bad mood, saying his back hurt and complaining about everything. Then the lights went down and the great curtain, thick with dust, was illuminated. The orchestra's driving music gave me goosepimples. Then, through the loudspeakers, a man introduced the show:

'...and tonight Versailles Special Productions are proud to present an outstanding programme of entertainments which we are sure you will enjoy. To begin with, please give a warm round of applause for that great radio success story, Enrique Tena...'

Tena was a flamenco singer who bounded onto the stage with a Cordobese hat in his hand. He acknowledged the audience with a deep bow and began to sing the story of an Englishman who wanted to learn to dance like him, but couldn't quite manage it...

'I say, do look, do look how I move my feet,' he went,

rhythmically tapping his heels as he moved across the stage. The people laughed and applauded.

'And now, just for you, the melodious voice that always touches the heart.'

It was a bolero singer who my mother liked a lot. Next there were some jugglers, a young singer who my father said had a bloody good voice, and a comic who always tripped up as he came on stage... The one that made the biggest impression on me was the human cannonball. He'd never played the Versailles before, and the compère explained the act in detail. We were going to see a man put himself in the barrel of a giant cannon, we'd hear a loud explosion and the man would fly over our heads to land, miraculously unharmed, in a net... All this, to drumrolls, brought about thunderous applause...

When we came out of the Versailles it was raining and my father put his jacket over my head. I felt like a midget with that enormous coat on... The streets were empty and we walked quickly, not saying anything, getting our feet wet. I felt a knot in my throat. Perhaps it hadn't been right to go to the Versailles with the boy dead; maybe we would never be able to go there again totally at ease... Because my socks had got wet too, after a while I started to shiver. If I get ill, I thought, maybe they won't send me to the island... Half way home my father let out a very loud fart.

'They'll hear you...' said my mother, embarrassed. She turned round to see if anyone was behind us.

'They can go fuck themselves...' said my father, quite simply.

But I didn't get ill and I went on with the same kind of life as ever. The only difference was that at school they said I was one of Ramon's arse-lickers, and they played tricks on me like knocking my inkwell over, putting glue on my chair, taking the nib off my pens or throwing bits of chalk at me while the teacher was writing on the board. They did it so well that they never got caught and the teacher thought it was me playing around, so he made me stand facing the wall with my arms crossed.

One day they tore a pocket on my smock. At home I said a boy had done it by accident when we were playing outside, but the truth is I didn't play during the breaks. I sat and watched the other kids. They ran around, kicked a ball, one would crouch while another put his hands on his back and leapt over, they talked to one another...

I was a little bit jealous of how easily they got along and the very open way they laughed, but it wasn't at all boring either watching their eyes: the one with blue eyes had very short hair, the brown-eyed one kept licking his lips, the one with the dark look had such big ears that he himself said that when he learned to move them he'd be able to fly... I observed the teachers as well: there was only one woman, who taught the youngest class, and the rest were men: the short tubby one who smoked yellow-papered cigarettes; the tall white-haired one who was always playing with his tie; a thin wrinkly man with a bow-tie who everyone called the wasted poet; the headmaster, who was bald and nervous, and practically all year round wore a dark hat tipped slightly to the right...

I liked watching and listening to people, but I never deduced anything from my observations. Ramon on the other hand used to tell exaggerated stories about each teacher. He said that the wasted poet sold paintings in an art gallery in the centre of Barcelona after school, the plump little one was an ex-policeman, that the one with the white hair was married to a woman with huge tits... He also claimed to have seen the little kids' teacher's knickers one day when he hid in the ladies' and she came in for a pee... All these things left me cold. I just liked watching them.

In fact I watched everything: the things in the classroom, the furniture at home, shop signs, the clothes people wore, haircuts, the trams, the cars... I could spend hours doing nothing, just contemplating what was around me. And in the summer, when we went out after dark to enjoy the cool air, I listened to the adults. I always had done. I found many of the things they said enigmatic:

'God, he looks like death warmed up.'

'When tomorrow comes.'

'It doesn't seem to hurt so much when I'm in bed...'

'What do you say to that...?'

'That woman's full of crocodile tears.'

I didn't know what crocodile tears meant, nor what it was that was hurting, but really the details were not important. The important thing was to keep in my mind these expressions that were so alive:

'Last night we said "Good evening" to Paco's widow.'

Things like that.

I also spent long periods watching my mother doing the housework when my father was out. If he wasn't around, my mother put the radio on. She liked listening to music and knew lots of songs by heart, which I'd hear her singing along to, very softly, following the voice of the singer. She didn't put it on so often when my father was at home, because according to him that contraption used a lot of electricity. It must have been true that the light was expensive, because sometimes they turned it off early and we had to have supper with paraffin lamps that gave off a little trail of smoke and smell.

'Bugger the lot of them...' muttered my father, annoyed, and my mother, from the kitchen, pretended she didn't understand.

'What did you say?'

'"Sod you," I said,' he replied. And then he gave me a fairly gentle clip on the ear. 'Eat...' But it was hard for me to swallow the boiled potatoes with a dash of oil that tasted only of boiled potatoes with a dash of oil. Sometimes, in the middle of supper, my father leaned to one side a little and let out a long noisy fart. We said nothing, but when the stink of rotten eggs got to me I frowned. 'What's wrong with you?' he said.

'Nothing,' I answered.

'Well, eat then.' But I wasn't hungry any more, and a little ball of potato started to form in my mouth; I chewed slowly, trying to keep it moist with saliva.

'Swallow...' said my mother after a while without looking at me, and I had to put this horrible pulp inside my body.

When I was in bed, in the dark, I also watched. These weren't dreams, nor my imaginings. I watched the silhouette of my hand, a reflection in the glass, little dots of light I could just make out on the ceiling, the mouths of the dead people who plagued me... And I watched my brother's face. Ramon was wrong. My brother was in heaven. What had it got to do with my brother, whatever my grandfather'd done? I didn't understand why he had got ill, didn't understand why he had had such a high fever, nor why he had died. What did die mean? It meant to stop living, but what was the difference between the one thing and the other? His heart stopped. But why did his heart stop? When they shot my grandfather, did his heart stop too? So it stopped for a different reason then? Couldn't it start up again? Why did my heart beat, while my brother's had stopped?

Sometimes in bed I cried in silence, biting my lip so no one would hear me. I didn't cry for my brother. I cried in torment, I cried over the potatoes with a dash of oil, my father's farts, the songs my mother sang almost clandestinely, the tricks they played on me at school, the grandiose red curtain of the Versailles, the comic who tripped up, the human cannonball and the moon, which always made my heart sink. It was so white, so round, so cold, so distant and out of reach... Love meant nothing. I loved lots of things. I loved my parents, and my brother, but that was nothing compared with the profound feeling of being alone in the world, of having been abandoned. I loved, and was loved, but I had nobody. I was like the moon, surrounded by stars but at the same time so alone and so sad. Except for the moon, I told myself as I was falling asleep, there was nothing. Everything around me faded away, became ethereal, fuzzy. The trees blurred into the mountain, the sand became an endless sea, unmoving and gluttonous, swallowing us. The boats were wiped away, the white villages where the fishermen lived, the houses, the lamps which lit the narrow streets, the streets themselves, the people... Then a cold fog fell over the school, obliterating the bricks, doors and windows, and the great bird of war flew past with its wings outstretched. The bird had red eyes and it gave me a sideways look, flapped its wings, and a hurricane wind grew out of the earth, a blazing storm which spiralled up to the sky like a golden column... Finally I fell asleep hearing distant explosions that could just as easily have been my father's farts as the bombs Joanet used to talk about when we spoke of the war. I heard shots, too, sharp brief reports that brought down the last shadows still standing...

I dreamt every night. Every night I relived my schoolmates' practical jokes, and every night I saw myself alone at the gates of a ruined fortress, trembling. I was the only person at a solemn funeral: the horses wore frozen mourning plumes and struggled to pull an icy black carriage, inside which there was a small white coffin that must have been incredibly heavy because the animals, puffing thick clouds of breath, could barely haul it along. I saw myself, insignificant behind the coach, my hands under my arms. It was cold and it proceeded so slowly that in fact the movement was imperceptible. The wheels broke the sheets of ice on the ground, and there wasn't enough night for the dream to fit in, not enough time for the long journey... However, an eternity later, the horses, the carriage, the coffin and I started to turn to the right. First the horses disappeared round the corner, and the hearse, with nobody in the driver's seat to steer it, also began to be swallowed up... Eventually the coffin too vanished, and to my surprise I couldn't follow it. I was left alone on that crossroads, lost, not knowing what was happening to me... Because suddenly I was in a street of bomb-shattered buildings, with few façades still standing, full of gashes and pockmarked by bullets where the stone had been splintered, the ground covered in dust... cloudy, grey. At the end of the street was a strange fire, which seemed painted, because the flames were only red, as deep as blood... Then nothing, a deep sleep, surrender.

The nights were dreadful, but so were the hours I spent at school. I only felt released when they rang the bell at the end of the day. They wouldn't push me any more in the assembly line, I wouldn't have to keep an eye on my crayons, which always went missing, the teacher wouldn't make me hold out my arm so he could hit the palm of my hand with a ruler... I always got home tired, not wanting to do my homework, and told my mother I didn't have any work to do and went out. First of all I went by the pulse shop and asked for Ramon. If he wasn't there I wandered around the streets for a while and ended up at Pere's Bar.

'What do you want?' said Ramon when he saw me, and I just looked at him.

Other times, when I couldn't find Ramon, I'd look for Joanet. At least Joanet told me things. One day he said that Perico had a serious problem. He'd been hired on a trial basis at a watchmaker's to see if he could go and work there after the summer, but after he'd been there a few days a pocket watch went missing. The owner accused him of stealing it. Perico said he hadn't touched a thing, as if he'd be crazy enough to do something like that... His father had to go and they were taken to the police, he was asked all sorts of questions, and he kept saying he'd never stolen anything from anyone. In the end the owner said he never wanted to see him around his shop again, and that he'd keep investigating.

'I would die if that happened to me...' said Joanet.

When I did come across Ramon, it was more fun. Ramon was resourceful, always knew a new place to hang out, had met some lads... Recently he'd been going a lot to a flat right next to the Ducal cinema. It was a flat the Falangists wanted to turn into a new local office, and for the moment it was almost empty. There were just some old tables, chairs and cardboard boxes full of propaganda and a few flags. The lad with the parting I'd seen playing table-football with Ramon was one of the ones who ran it, but there wasn't any problem getting in because until its opening, the key was always in the door. I was scared of going to the flat, but apparently in the first few days almost all the kids in the street went, including Antonio, Perico, Jaume and Joanet, Salvador, Miquel. They didn't do anything special, sat on the floor, talked, smoked, moved around boxes and furniture... In one of the rooms, the biggest, there was a photograph of Franco and one of Jose Antonio. They'd given out papers which explained who Jose Antonio was, and also, because Perico had explained the events at the watchmaker's, they said they'd have a word with the owner and not to worry. I'd heard about all this but I didn't go to the flat because I knew that priests and the Falange were not at all popular at home. No one could say as much, but at home they weren't liked, and the best thing was to keep away from them, according to my mother.

'You say you know nothing, always say you know nothing...' she advised. And, more or less, I did what she said.

But one afternoon Ramon dragged everyone down to the flat, and when I said I didn't want to go he told me I was a coward.

'If I ever see you within ten yards of me again, I'll rearrange your face,' Ramon warned me. Luckily, though, when the whole group of us went down to Poblenou beach a few days later he'd forgotten.

I couldn't tell my mother I was going so far, nor that we were going past the open sewer at Bogatell. The water that flowed down there stank terribly; it was thick as lead, greenish and full of bottles and garbage. According to Antonio, if you fell in that channel, you were done for. Among us was Salvador, who was my age, but tall, with curly hair. His father was chauffeur to a bank manager, and they seemed rich, because they lived in a two-storey house with a garden. He went to a different school, a religious one, and when he came along with us he always said the same thing: his father this and his father that, he wanted to study to be a draughtsman... Also there was Jaume, who was subhuman as only he could be. When he knew his mother was making lentils, he used to collect little pebbles off the street and, behind her back, put them in the pot at dinner time. The woman went spare, saying she had cleaned them really well, that she didn't understand it at all... And then Miquel, who was all holy, went to communion on Sundays, and complained about the way we talked. Maybe there were even more people. This trip was one of the big events that Ramon organised. He looked pleased with himself, going ahead of us, and the only one who moaned was Perico, who had to be careful because of his leg.

When we got to the beach we lay down on the sand, with our clothes on. There was nobody else there apart from us, but it still wasn't warm enough to bathe in our underpants. What's more, around there the water was disgusting because that's where the sewer emptied out. With the wash of the waves, the sand was covered in scum and all sorts of rubbish. All the same I liked the constant murmur of the sea.

'If we go up there,' said Ramon pointing over to the left, 'we'll come across the gypsy shacks. Who's coming?'

There was a lot of indecision. Miquel said he wanted nothing to do with it, at all, but he wasn't going home on his own either; Salvador, Antonio, Jaume and Perico said yes immediately, and Joanet and I said nothing... In the end we all went off to the shacks. Salvador said that it wasn't only gypsies who live there, there were people 'hiding from the police', maybe reds, people who since the war hadn't left the labyrinth of wooden houses, shacks put together in a hurry, covered with corrugated iron and bits of asbestos scavenged off building sites.

To begin with we walked a fair way down the beach, at the water's edge, and then crossed through a gap in a wall of clay bricks that gave on to some waste land at the bottom of which was the railway line. Then, to our right, between the railway tracks and the sand, we saw this different, terrible world.

When we got there, Antonio pointed out right at the entrance a bar where, according to him, they did very good grilled sardines. And, as if he knew exactly where he was taking us, he led us in among the shacks. I was surprised to see how the people were washing clothes in the street, children playing in puddles of dirty water, a group of swarthy men surrounding a brazier, burning piles of electric cable which gave off black smelly smoke that spread through the dwellings. The women wore long dresses down to their feet and big aprons. Most of the men were ill-shaven and their hands were dirty.

'They're poorer than we are...' said Joanet in my ear, and he was right.

Finally we stopped at the entrance to a shack where Ramon and Perico started talking with a dyed-blonde woman who didn't look gypsy. From what I could gather, they knew her, and she sold them tobacco. Then we saw a fat woman, sleeping in the street in an armchair with no legs, and some lads, bare chested, no shirts or vests, sitting in a circle clapping. Further on there was an old man with a very dark face, his lips purple, watching us...

Out the other side of the shacks we came to the beach again, which was even dirtier than by the sewer. Despite that, there were boats which these people took out to catch fish they then sold at the market in buckets, without any permits or anything. My mother sometimes bought some of it because it was cheaper than in the shops, but she would never have even dreamed that I had been to where the gypsies lived.

'What's up?' asked Ramon at one point.

'Nothing...' I replied.

'Well you look scared shitless...'

On the way home, he kept making fun of me, saying I'd been afraid, that I was a pile of shit, and wondering out loud what would have happened if they'd taken me down to the whore-house...

'You don't even know what a cunt looks like, do you,' he said, laughing.

When my father got ill, my mother got a real fright. He was always whining, saying that at home he never got any respect, all he was good for was to graft away like a dog, to do all the donkey work and that the day he wasn't around they'd soon see what had hit them... We were used to his exaggerations, but we also knew that when he took to his bed, ashen-faced, and asking to see his sisters, that something was really up.

We rarely saw his sisters, and even less his half-brother Uncle Sebastià. They were very different from us and Uncle Pere; they lived in big apartments full of furniture, and my aunties even had telephones and maids. To me they were strange ladies who always wore makeup and were uncomfortable around us. When the boy died, my aunties apparently lent us money for the funeral, but according to my mother they had to hand over their wedding rings as surety. If this subject ever came up my father immediately went up the wall, screaming inches from my mother's ear that it was a lie, a lie, that she was just jealous of his sisters, that it had been he who had given them the rings because he didn't want charity from them, that they hadn't wanted to take them and he'd had to really insist...

'Do you hear?' he yelled. 'I had to insist a lot... a lot!' he repeated over and over, pushing and shoving at her.

I don't know. We saw them sometimes, at the odd christening, funerals or perhaps on Boxing Day, which was when Auntie Carme invited us to coffee. They had only been to our house a couple of times, and in fact I only remember seeing them there when the boy died, all remorseful and bemoaning the fact that we had to live in that shack, as they called it.

'When this is all over, you get yourselves an apartment... We'll help you with it,' they said to my father. But afterwards there was never any more talk of that.

I didn't think of the house we lived in as a shack. It was true we didn't have running water and in winter it was freezing cold; that it leaked, that the walls ran with damp, and in summer the bedrooms were like furnaces, but compared to where the gypsies lived it wasn't a shack. My mother kept everything clean and tidy, and in any case our single storey was the same as all the other houses in our street. In some respects it was better than the others because we had a big courtyard where we had our supper in the summertime, but my aunties didn't like it.

'There's no need for you to live like that...' they said to my father. And when his sisters weren't there, he would mutter, 'They really get on my tits, going on about the house like that.' But he said nothing to their faces.

As well as Aunt Carme and Aunt Mercè, there was Auntie Lourdes, who didn't do so much with the family because, it was said, she lived with a married man. I'd only met her a few times, but I'd heard she was the nicest of the three of them, and that she couldn't even look at her sisters in a picture.

'Carme pretends,' my mother said to Aunt Neli from time to time, 'that Lourdes doesn't even exist, but in fact she isn't fit to lick her boots.'

Auntie Mercè, for all the grand airs she exuded, was really foul-mouthed, but in this respect I liked her, because she let fly the curses and swearwords so naturally. One time the maid spilled a little bit of coffee from the cup as she was serving her, and she said, 'Why don't you just pour it straight down my fanny?' Her husband, Uncle Ramon, had an engine factory, and was bald and always kept quiet but on that occasion he did say that it wasn't right to talk like that at table. She replied if he didn't like her way of doing things he could leave right there and then. 'And you know what?' she added. 'You can stick it up your arse and smoke it.'

She always left lipstick on the cup and I was intrigued by her long curved nails which seemed to grow on her like weapons. She had dyed blond hair, painted dark wide eyebrows, wore mascara on her lashes, was pretty hefty and had immense breasts that wobbled like blancmanges when she wore a low-cut dress.

Aunt Carme was different. She had dark, well groomed hair, white skin, and was said to be ill. It must have been because of her poor health that she always seemed far away and sad. Despite this, at times her eyes fired up, and out would come the family's nastiness. They lived in a big house in Castelldefels and her husband, Uncle Esteve, was always elegantly dressed, in double-breasted jacket and gold watch. According to my father, Uncle Esteve was really nice, earned as much money as he wanted, and didn't skimp on high-class hookers that cost him an arm and a leg. They had a daughter, Imma, who was older than us and had English lessons.

Uncle Sebastià was only their brother through the mother, and everyone thought he was a very clever man. He had white hair, wore glasses and lived in an imposingly dark flat with lots of curtains. We had been to see them once or twice, and his wife had greeted my mother with a kiss, put a hand on my head and then led us in down a never-ending corridor. My uncle received us in a room full of armchairs, little tables, and lamps that were always lit.

'Sit down,' he said. And she brought biscuits and coffee.

I felt great admiration for this small-eyed man who listened without speaking and tended to come up with solutions that nobody had thought of. He was like a kind of guarantee, and so we went to see him when anything serious went wrong. I recall him one day, during one of these visits, fixing his eye on me.

'And you,' he said, 'what do you want to study?'

It was the first time he had ever spoken to me, and I, unnerved, replied that I didn't know. I'd never thought of studying anything. I was a street lad, just one of the gang, like Perico, Antonio, Joanet, Jaume... We didn't study, we went to school, we played, and when the time came we would work somewhere or other, then we'd do military service... Just like everyone else. All this about studying was new. At school they didn't even talk to me about it. They'd sooner tell me my handwriting was bad, that I never listened, that I was distant...

'You're like a stone,' the wasted poet teacher had said to me, rapping his knuckles on my head. 'Hard as stone...'

In a way he was right, but for them to say these things hurt me more than the blows. It was like with Ramon, who

33

made fun of the boy's death for no reason, saying the boy couldn't have gone to heaven. How did he know he wasn't in heaven? Who told him? 'The world,' I ruminated, 'is full of unjust people, who will say things to hurt others for no reason.' Then I clammed up and put up with it, because that was all I knew how to do. But inside me, deep inside, somewhere inaccessible, there was a little light that comforted me. I'll manage to reach that light, I told myself with my eyes closed, concentrating as hard as I could, clenching my fists to get me closer to it. I'll get there and then there'll be justice. I didn't tell myself this in so many words, but the meaning was clear, and it let me endure the uncertainty brought about by unexpected questions, contempt and indifference.

Precisely because of all this – the light, what people thought of me, the poverty we lived in – I had to keep watching the others, stay alert, looking and listening... I didn't know what would happen when I left school. Sometimes my mother said I would be a mechanic. At others she suggested I should go and work in a factory, without specifying at all what I would do there or what sort of factory she meant. I'd also heard the best thing was to learn a trade, any trade, because then you always had work. And I, looking at her, wondered to myself why couldn't I just die like my brother... It wasn't an unpleasant idea. Close my eyes, sleep for ever, not breathe any more, forget everything, plunge into a dark silence like the one that fell on the streets when the sun went down... And if death was like that, why were we so afraid of it? Why did they talk about my grandfather and my brother out of my earshot? I wasn't frightened to let myself go down that dark slope. I was more frightened that they would send me to Menorca to live with those people I didn't know. Better to stay still, catching glimpses of the faint distant flame I could just make out at the end of the huge blackness.

As I was saying, my father took to his bed, moaning all the time and gripping my hand tightly, and then he wanted us to tell his sisters and Uncle Sebastià, which got my mother very scared.

'I don't know what's wrong with me...' muttered my father, his lips colourless, putting his hands to the small of his back, 'I don't know what's wrong...'

It was spring and it was raining those big warm drops I liked so much. My mother had gone twice to telephone the doctor from Mrs Palmira's shop and had also called my aunts and Sebastià. But only Aunts Carme and Mercè came.

'What's wrong with my brother?' asked Auntie Mercè, flustered, as she put her umbrella down on the table. My mother replied that his back was hurting, that she'd called the doctor, and that she didn't know what to do. 'Clearly, my dear,' muttered Mercè to my mother, 'you're useless.' And, mind made up, she went into the room.

After a while we were all sitting around my father's bed: my mother, me, Auntie Carme who also didn't look very well, and Aunt Mercè, who was wearing a narrow skirt. As her feet had got wet, she first took off her shoes and then her stockings because she said the damp wasn't at all good for her. I was very struck to see how the skirt rode up and she showed off her thighs just like that, thighs that seemed to me enormous and very white. Meanwhile my father was groaning, rolling his eyes, holding his hands to his kidneys and asking if they'd told Sebastià. They told him they had, and he leant his head to one side with a sigh, as if he wanted to rest. My mother went into the kitchen to hang out my aunt's stockings and then Mercè asked my father if he had eaten anything. He said no with a shake of his head.

'Don't scare us,' said Carme. 'We've got enough trouble as it is...'

While they looked to see if my father had a fever, my mother prepared lemon and water for my aunts, who remained seated by the bed, beside my father, who had fallen asleep. My mother was anxious because the doctor hadn't come and she didn't know what to say to her sisters-in-law. She came and went, ran her fingers through my hair... One of those nights when my father had started shouting, and ended up slamming the door and going off to the bar, my mother had come to my side crying and also touched my hair. Then, very softly, she said she had always been unlucky, she didn't remember her mother, grandfather had died too young, she'd had to go out to work straight away, when she met my father she never thought it would go the way it did, during the war she'd been very hungry, that dreadful shooting, the business with the boy... She told me she would rather never have left the island, that she only had me. Sometimes I felt a great tenderness towards my mother. I saw her as vulnerable, fragile, lost in a world that wasn't hers, but didn't know what to do. Maybe she wanted to take me off to the island because she thought that was best for me, get me away from my aunts and the kids in the streets, make me change my life... Or maybe it was my father who wanted me to go...

I wanted to get out of the house and fortunately, because it had stopped raining and my aunts had started talking to each other as if we weren't there, my mother told me I might as well go out and play for a while. I ran out, not knowing where to go, but glad to leave behind the confined atmosphere of the little room and the conversations I didn't understand. At that time of day, I said to myself, the others could only be at Pere's Bar or the Falangist flat which, while it hadn't quite been fully set up, Ramon had made his own. Ramon, Antonio and Perico had become obsessed with the story of the watchmaker's; they said they wanted to sort out the owner, that the Falangists would go over and talk to him to put the fear of God into him and if they had to they'd break his shop-window. Joanet had told me that sometimes the three of them would climb up the back of a tram so they didn't have to pay and go along until the conductor saw them and shouted at them to get off while it was still moving. Then they would explode into laughter and had something to talk about for the whole afternoon. They had also met some strange people who lived three or four streets up, an old woman and an old man whose house they sometimes went to. They were very dirty according to Joanet, had a grown-up son and shared the house with a sort of giant, a very tall man whose legs were so swollen he could hardly walk... They did everything like this, Ramon, Antonio and Perico, going from one thing to another...

In the evening, when I got home, my mother told me the doctor had been, that my father didn't have anything serious, a torn muscle, and that he had to rest. And because he was in bed, dozing, the two of us had supper on our own, with the radio on, very low so as not to disturb him. My mother seemed happy, liberated, and she let me eat just the beans and leave the potatoes.

I also learned about the life we led at home when I came to know those old people whom Ramon, Antonio and Perico had come across in a house similar to mine but more dilapidated, without electricity and full of odd sticks of furniture, piles of newspapers, books, a pair of cats and a white dog who sniffed my feet and legs the first day he saw me. I was taken there by the lads from the gang, and according to Joanet who came too, I'd be amazed at the shit there was in the house and the things the old people did. The woman, Mrs Rosalia, had one eye completely sunken, so sunken you could hardly see it, and hair the colour of ash that she had cut to ear level as if she was a prince in a storybook... Mr Gaspar, her husband, I recall being very thin, in a double-breasted jacket and a cigarette always between his lips. They had a son, César, twenty-something years old, quite chubby. And then there was Edir, the giant, who really was very tall and had trouble walking. Occasionally a married daughter appeared with her husband, who was slim, bald, and wore glasses with thick lenses.

The lads in the gang only went there for a laugh, to spy on the old lady who they said sometimes went and peed standing up in the middle of the yard, and Edir, the giant who also amused them because he was usually sitting in an armchair right at the doorway to the house, and when he saw them would salute by raising his arm, like the Falangists. Then, if they spoke to him, he'd start mumbling a song in English until, from his seat, he'd grab a sepia-coloured newspaper off a pile he had next to the armchair and violently hurl it at them.

'They say the newspaper's in English, too,' said Joanet. 'What do you make of that...?'

But what they thought was funniest about this man was that he often fell asleep with his flies undone, and because he hadn't washed in years according to Ramon, a cloud of black frenzied insects would quickly form. Ramon also said that from time to time Edir was visited by a young well-dressed woman who sat by him and talked to him for a while with her legs slightly apart. To begin with, the giant took her by the hand, but then tried to touch her thighs under her dress until she told him off saying that was enough of that. When the boys in the group looked at her, she smiled at them, and, mocking, said that if they behaved themselves next time she'd bring them sweets. The giant got cross, but bit by bit he got used to seeing them around and then barely took any notice.

The first day I was dumbstruck. It was true they were very dirty folk and the house was very run down. Just stepping into the yard – the old woman called it the garden – you realised there were half-disintegrated cardboard boxes full of broken bottles at the back, a rusty bicycle frame with no wheels, heaps of worm-eaten bits of wood, dog shit, old wire, mangled birdcages and bushes of all sorts... The door to the house was always open, and inside you could just make out the dark flaking walls. On the right, an arm's length from the entrance, was where the giant lived, almost always sitting in the armchair, reading newspapers or sleeping. On the left there was a kitchen, where the cats wandered over the range, sniffing into corners. Further inside, Antonio told me that first day, there was a dining table and a bunk for the son, and right at the end the little boxroom where the old people slept. At that point I could not even begin to suspect that thanks to these people I would, for the first time, see the bright light which until then I had only imagined.

In fact, the first visit got off to a problematic start because of Ramon. We got there in the middle of the afternoon, when it was still light, and because all we could see was Edir, sleeping in his armchair, we entered down the side of the yard under the bedroom windows, with the toilet right at the bottom.

'The shit,' said Ramon in a low voice, 'ends up in a cesspit. You see that manhole cover? Well, every so often they lift it up, put in big pipes, iron ones, that they connect up to a truck, and all the way from the street it sucks everything out till the pit's empty. It makes a hell of a noise when the shit goes down it, and if you put your ear right up against the tube you can hear all the crap and piss running through... It's absolutely brilliant...'

Then, as Ramon was explaining all about the toilet, the window of the old people's room opened, and Mr Gaspar, really annoyed, screamed threateningly that we were morons and that he had had it up to here with us disturbing them.

'What is it?' yelled the old lady from inside, very agitated.

'Nothing,' he shouted back. 'Just those pain in the arse kids.'

'Oh, forget them,' she said dismissively.

Antonio and Ramon started to run off, but Perico, Jaume, Joanet and I stayed rooted to the spot. When he slammed the window shut, we went warily to the front yard, unable to repress a nervous sort of laughter that made Joanet want to pee. As we went past the door, Gaspar's son, César, appeared with a book in his hand, and Perico, with bare-faced cheek, told him Joanet needed to go to the toilet but had a thing about going on his own so that's why we were going with him. The old man then came out as if nothing was going on, lighting a cigarette, the dog following him, and César explained about Joanet. But the old man disappeared without replying. Edir went on sleeping, and then César started to stroke the dog, whose name was Sultan. A little later César sat down on a bench and asked us if we liked reading.

'Reading?' asked Joanet defensively. 'How do you mean?'

'You're right,' said César with a friendly smile. 'You can read many things, but I'm talking about literature.'

'I don't know,' replied Joanet, and César made an effort to explain himself better:

'Literature, novels, poems... That's what I like most,' and then we knew what he was talking about.

'We only read school books,' said Perico.

'That's different...' César explained. 'I didn't go to school much, and the truth is I didn't really like it at all.'

'We don't like it either,' said Joanet.

'Okay, but it's good to go.'

'Yes,' added Perico, 'but soon I'll be going to work, and school won't do me any good then.'

'Well, you never know,' said César. 'If I'd studied, I'd be able to work at whatever I liked now, instead of...'

Perico asked him what he did for a living and he explained that he did a bit of everything; sometimes he delivered things in a van, he'd been a labourer in a factory, and he'd also worked in a watchmaker's...

'Christ,' let out Perico, and we all started laughing.

César wanted to know what we were laughing at, and when Perico related his story, the man listened attentively. From time to time he nodded his head in agreement. We, Perico, Joanet, Jaume and I, were used to people asking us questions and answering them, but we'd never talked for such a long time with an adult. César treated us as if we were the same age as him, didn't order us around at all, listened to Perico explain the accusations against him and seemed to side with him. So there we were, sitting on the ground around César, and we went on chatting about work, about how difficult it was to get along with foremen and bosses, the differences that existed between people who had money and those that didn't... I still hadn't said anything, but because I could see that I could contribute whenever I wanted, and I wouldn't be told to shut up, I said, without thinking, 'My aunts have got lots of money. Not all my aunts, just two of them, and an uncle who reads a lot too... and it's true, they're not like us.'

'Of course,' said César, 'these sorts of differences can occur within families. And if you ever need to ask them for anything, the ones with the money, then that's bad news.'

'My father,' I added, more sure of myself, 'says he doesn't want charity from people.'

'He's right,' said César. 'And you know what happens? You always end up giving them back more than they've lent you.'

That day even Perico was talking seriously. None of us had ever taken part in a conversation like this. Joanet seemed fascinated and started laughing, joyful, when I started to tell stories about my aunts. At one point he said, 'Shit, you tell it really well! They're the old bag aunties from hell!' and we all shat ourselves laughing.

I liked being listened to; I liked making them laugh, having things to say, and it seemed unreal being able to participate in a conversation, just like that... It was different from when we met up in summertime, going out round the streets after supper. I used to listen, but deep down nothing they said interested me. On the other hand, with César, it was as if time stood still, as if none of us had anything more important to do than talk naturally about these inconsequential things.

Later on, César explained to us what the book he was reading was about. It was the story of a very poor student who decides to kill a contemptible old woman who lends money on extortionate terms. The student kills her because he is convinced the crime is justifiable since it allows him to develop his vocation and help others. In time he meets a young prostitute to whom he confesses his crime, and, slowly, remorse and doubt begin to mortify him. At the same time, the police are closing the ring around him...

'Do they get him in the end?' asked Perico, all curiosity. To which César replied that they did.

'What a bummer...' said Joanet, watching Perico and seeing him more thoughtful than usual.

'That depends how you look at it,' César went on. 'In fact he himself helps the police solve the crime. It's not that he feels entirely guilty, rather that he seeks a kind of redemption. He has to carry out a sublime act, different from anything anybody else has done... Do you understand?'

'Yes,' replied Joanet, and then he asked if he'd read the whole book, and César replied that he had, he'd read it twice, and was reading it once again.

'But if you already know the ending...' said Perico.

'That's not important,' explained César. 'What matters is the way the writer uncovers the student's mind, the ultimate meaning of the crime, and the need for punishment, of one kind or another. But I'm not talking about the punishment of the police or society. It's something else which is perhaps more difficult to explain. But you don't have to reread the book because it's difficult to understand; it's that each time you go back to it you like it more than the last time because you discover new angles.'

'Bloody hell,' said Perico, 'you really do know stuff...'

'No,' said César. 'I already told you I didn't go to school much. But it's true that reading makes you see everything differently.'

'With me, I just get tired of it,' said Jaume, and César explained to him that that only happened at the beginning and later you'd never stop reading because each book fills you with lives that otherwise you'd never know.

That afternoon's conversation, which to me seemed fascinating and unrepeatable, stayed in my head all night. I did what César had done with the book about the poor student: I went over and over what each of us had said, enjoyed the gentle way this man who we'd never met before had spoken to us. And, just as he'd told us, it was true that by going over things you could understand them better. It seemed to me, for example, that maybe Perico had stolen that watch. I wasn't sure, but the questions he asked, the way he'd lowered his eyes when we were talking about punishment... Perhaps it wasn't as I imagined it, but anyway, if he had done it, I wouldn't think of him as less of a friend; perhaps as even more of a friend than before. After all, Perico was lame, he was one of us, and who's to say he didn't have a right to that watch. Neither did it seem to me that César was telling us that we should steal and kill to get what we wanted. That's not what he'd said. He'd showed us that through the fault of others, a soul can come to torture itself, even while believing it had acted correctly.

When I went to sleep, my head was going round and round, and at midnight, sweaty and troubled, I was woken by my father's snoring. From time to time I could hear the creak of the bed as he moved. Through the window I could see a fragment of dark sky and lots of little white motionless dots; no one had ever been able to explain to me why they were there. For sure, if I'd dared go out to the yard I'd have seen the moon too, but I didn't go because my mother would

44

have woken up and if I'd told her I was going to look at the moon, she'd have taken a slipper to me. Anyway, with my eyes closed, I could see an enormous yellow moon, surrounded by thousands and thousands of stars, more than I had ever seen. And I saw the darkness, the darkness which had always drawn me. In an unreachable corner of this endless darkness, far away, there was my brother, looking at me. Maybe my grandparents and all the other dead people were there too. I sent my brother a kiss, and hugging the pillow, I calmly let sleep carry me away.

Afterwards, for several days our group talked almost exclusively about how the conversation with César had gone. Ramon was scornful and said he wasn't going back to the old people's house, that he didn't want people boiling his brains with nonsense about poofter old lady killers. We talked to Salvador about it, because his father had books, and to Miquel and Antonio, who thought the same as Ramon.

'If he kills the old lady, he kills her, and that's that...' was Antonio's conclusion.

Later Jaume suggested going to see the girls coming out of school. He'd met one who was older than him and went to a convent school. 'Her name's Montse, and maybe she'll even let you play with her tits...' he said.

'But she hasn't got any,' said Perico, who was older, and reckoned he knew about these things.

'What do you mean she hasn't got any?' said Jaume. 'I bet they wouldn't fit in your hand... They must be this big...'

At school, everything continued as before. Perhaps the only new thing was that since I'd been going out more with the group they didn't try to wind me up so much. There was also a bit of commotion when we found out that the police had picked up the father of a boy called Daniel. They'd turned up at his house in the night, kicked at the door, violently, and when his mother opened it, terrified, they just shoved her aside. According to Daniel, when his father came out in his underwear to see what was happening, one of the policemen landed him a dreadful smack in the face, right in front of his mother. Daniel had got up and saw it all too. They went into the bedroom to see if anybody else was there, threw his trousers at him, dragged him out to the yard and said they were taking him away. Daniel wasn't in school for a few days, and eventually his mother had to go and talk to the teachers. Daniel's father was locked up in prison and they started to go hungry because they didn't have two halfpennies to rub together. Neighbours apparently took them food, and one day, at home, there was a row when my father went mad shouting at my mother that she was brainless and shouldn't take food to anyone, that in our situation there was no way we could get involved in any of this shit, we'd already had a bad enough time of it... My mother didn't know what to say, remarking that she'd only lent them some vegetables and rice and would never do it again...

All of this was discussed even when we went for supper at Uncle Pere and Aunt Neli's house. In this respect, things had been going well for some time, and when my father and uncle saw each other they didn't quarrel. I took more notice of my cousins, especially Esther, who had started work as an assistant in a clothes shop and sometimes put make-up on her eyes. My uncle viewed her disparagingly, saying she looked like a tart and would end up like Aunt Lourdes, and then she ran off crying to her room, unable to reply. My other cousin,

Lola, was my age and had very curly hair. She was always playing with dolls, hardly spoke, and when I looked at her just stuck her tongue out at me.

These suppers at my uncle's house always started off the same. Out of the blue my father said to my mother we were going to have supper at his brother's house, my mother said she didn't have anything made, he said to just make anything. She then hurriedly made some omelettes, grabbed some tomatoes and bread and put it all in a basket. We went on foot usually. They didn't live far away, but it was tiring going at my father's pace, him walking in front of us as if he was in a foul mood. Sometimes he turned round and said to my mother, who was carrying the basket, 'What are you waiting for?' and my mother replied that he was walking too fast.

'Bollocks I'm walking too fast,' he said and started walking faster than before. When we finally got there, Aunt Neli pretended she was happy.

In contrast Uncle Pere, watering the pots on the balcony, was saying, very quietly, things like, 'The more the merrier...'

'How are you doing?' said my father. Uncle Pere replied he was fine, and if things were all right between them, as they were just then, that was that.

Then they talked about the case of Daniel's father, who had the same name. They'd beaten the shit out of him, he was in a really bad way, they said his face was all smashed up, he'd rot in prison, poor man, what'll his wife and son do now, they're marked for life, they'll have a really hard time of it, it's madness to get involved in anything political... These were all separate sentences, not a conversation like Perico, Joanet, Jaume and I had had with César. Anyway, I realised that this business with Daniel was serious, and though I hadn't wanted to think about it, my grandfather came to mind, that that was how he'd been killed. I didn't dare ask what my grandfather had done, nor why they'd shot him, but I deduced that during the war he'd got involved in things to do with the anarchists.

These suppers made me feel sad. They talked a lot about Aunt Lourdes, Aunt Carme, Mercè and Sebastià. Uncle Esteve had bought himself a radiogram, they said, Carme was feeling a little better, and they'd even seen her smile. There was something or other about Uncle Ramon, too... On the other hand Mercè was as miserable a cow as ever. They hadn't heard from Sebastià for a while...

'He's like a shadow...' said Uncle Pere, in Spanish, swallowing his voice and opening his eyes like Luis Sandrini. 'Sebastià is like a shadow...'

Aunt Neli was always nervous, doing three or four things at the same time, and could never sit still, saying she was the one who was stuffed and not Carme, and it was unreal how they could earn so much money...

All this slid straight past me without affecting me. It was like at school, I didn't understand what they were saying and I didn't want to understand it either. Sometimes my aunt said she'd had a letter from Menorca and apparently they were asking when they were going to go, and they seemed well... Then I did listen attentively. Menorca was a mystery from many points of view. I'd never been there, but at home they always said one summer we'd go, when we had a bit of money. And then there was all that about me going there, which occasionally came back into my mind and worried me, but because the days were long, it wasn't cold, I was doing better with the boys in the group, and there weren't any big fights, I had also slightly forgotten about it.

From One World to the Other

Then suddenly something happened, which I remember vaguely, in black and white, full of noises and movements that never quite fit together. Just like my father used to say, it really did seem we'd never be able to hold our heads up high, as if since the war had ended, all we ever got was tragedy. This bastard bad luck had grabbed us by the throat, he'd say, forever biting, savaging us. We could count our blessings, my mother said later, that we'd never been through anything like this ourselves...

At home one night, we too got a violent knock on the door. We heard a voice shouting for my father: it was Uncle Pere, and my parents rushed to undo the bolt. I sat up in bed and could hear them perfectly, and despite all the confusion I realised that we had been hit once again by the same tidal wave that had struck us before. I felt completely paralysed. Absolute helplessness that prevented me from getting up, or thinking, or reacting in any way at all. I'd never heard Uncle Pere talk like this before either, beside himself, unnerved, deeply serious. He and his wry, sardonic detachment...

'Esteve's been killed in the car!' he was shouting. 'He's been killed!'

I'm not sure how I knew this, because I was in my bed, but I'm sure my uncle was smacking his hands against his forehead. I'd seen him do this before when things got too much for him: he'd open up his hands and smack the palms against his forehead. Aunt Neli would tell him he was crazy and his brains would burst, but he never took any notice and kept smacking his forehead until it was really red... Well, I think that's what he did that night. I pictured him hitting himself like that, screaming that Esteve'd been killed in the car, and my father colourless, as he always went when he got scared, my mother with her hands to her mouth, saying nothing.

'Bloody hell!' my uncle yelled. 'I don't believe it! I don't believe it!'

Then, I'm not sure how, they told me to get dressed, that my uncle had had an accident, and in the middle of the night we went out onto the street.

The streets were empty, black, calm. There were no cars about, and the four of us started walking quickly towards Uncle Pere's house. My father's face was completely white. My mother had put on a skirt that I thought was longer than usual. I was wearing a light shirt and dark trousers. There was no light at the windows of the houses. There was a small moon, and only a few stars.

'Young Esther's gone to look for a taxi,' my uncle said as we walked.

'Is it going to take us to Castelldefels?' asked my mother a little later.

'I suppose so...' my uncle replied.

It was strange making our way through this peace in the streets, crushed by the tragedy. Maybe I hadn't fully realised exactly what was happening, but I felt that somehow death was ferociously hunting us down. Besides that, wherever you looked, everything was ugly, sordid and lightless. Daniel's father in prison, Perico's bad leg, those corpses in the hospital, the filth in the house where Cèsar lived, the sickly look in Miquel's face all the time because he went to Mass so much, Joanet's problems, people who'd lost relatives in the war... Now Uncle Esteve, I said to myself, he's been killed in the car... I wondered what it meant, that he'd been killed in the car. Where had all this happened? How had Uncle Pere got to hear about it? I knew that all these questions had simple answers, but I felt I didn't have it in me to come up with them. I remember very clearly thinking that living was like being in a boat and rowing against the tide. A violent river of black water dragging us one way and us struggling against it. There were moments of calm, not many, but there were some. Sometimes everything was full, sometimes everything was empty. I remembered eating bitter fruit that I'd had to spit out, and then a bunch of cherries as dark as blood and sweet as honey. I felt a great weight in my eyes, of sleep most probably, as I thought these things, and when we got to my uncle's house it was heavier than ever. I remembered the student in that book César had told us about. His predicament was very difficult. Deep down, he felt guilty because other people made him feel guilty by regarding his crime as punishable. The student was really feeling the weight of society rather than his own remorse... Anyway, as we walked along, this was the sort of thing I thought about. Guilt, difficulties, weariness, indifference... The truth is I felt no urge to cry, not in the slightest; I simply felt weariness and sadness.

When we got to the corner where my uncle lived, we saw my cousin Esther, who suddenly put her arm up. Just beyond there was a big taxi with its doors open. The driver had got out and was standing there waiting, talking to the local watchman. Also suddenly, as if they'd been told to, out of the doorway came Aunt Neli and my cousin Lola. They seemed to be hurrying out, rather like shadows, but maybe I was imagining that. It also seemed that there was a group of them, but in fact it was just the two. I don't remember any sound, or any voice disturbing the silence in the street except Esther, who gave me a kiss on the cheek when she saw me, and murmured 'Hello.'

The watchman opened out the taxi's folding seats, and bit by bit, procession-like, we all got in. Uncle Pere was in the front beside the driver. My father and Aunt Neli sat in the dickey seats and my mother and us kids, Esther, Lola and I, settled into the back seat. I felt I could see the taxi drive away. In other words, the watchman was left standing there in the middle of the street, hat on head, and it seemed that I was looking at the taxi going off in exactly the way he was: a single point of colour fading away in the night.

I'd never been in a taxi for such a long time, and never on the open road. But first we went through sleeping streets. I saw a man walking close up by a wall. I also saw the taxi from that man's point of view. It could only be bad news, a taxi full of people at that time of night... My father lit a cigarette. He filled his lungs with smoke and expelled it slowly. He and I caught each other's eye momentarily, without speaking. I will always remember the clear look in his eyes that night. My mother squeezed herself into the corner to give us more room. Aunt Neli, twisting herself round, looked out the front.

'Lucky we found you, isn't it?' said my aunt to the driver.

'Shame about why though...' he replied.

'You're telling me...' my aunt answered.

Out on the open road the car started going faster and it felt as if we were being sucked into a gorge of blackness. My uncle and the driver spoke for a moment. My uncle said that when we got to Castelldefels he would give directions.

Then the driver lit a cigarette.

'Are we nearly there?' asked Lola sleepily after a while.

'Any minute now,' said my aunt.

We were all a little calmer. I may have fallen asleep. I had a sense of vertigo, on the edge of a bottomless void. When we got to my aunt's house we found out that my uncle had been out to eat with a friend of his. On the way back, nearly home, he lost control of the vehicle and it went over the edge of a sharp drop and smashed into a tree. The man he was with was able to get out of the car, and went back up to the road to call for help. He only had a few cuts on his face and hands, but my uncle's chest was impaled on the steering wheel and he died there and then, and there was nothing anyone could do.

The day of the funeral, Uncle Sebastià sat between Aunt Carme and my cousin Imma. Because she wasn't well, my aunt had been given medicine that made her really drowsy. Both of them cried a lot, my father too, and Uncle Pere, and Aunt Neli, and my mother, Aunt Mercè, Uncle Ramon and Aunt Lourdes who had been reconciled with the family over this. Nobody could have predicted anything so awful, even less that it should happen to them, because they were always lucky people for whom nothing ever went wrong.

But after the funeral, everyone still devastated by the bereavement, it turned out that things weren't as clear as they'd seemed. The house they lived in was mortgaged, they spent too much money from day to day and had nothing saved, so without the income my uncle had been getting from who knows where, everything would have to change. Uncle Sebastià took charge of affairs and met several times at his house with the brothers and sisters, apart from Aunt Carme, who wasn't able to think about much at all.

At one of these meetings, he explained that he had spoken to the bank, who had examined the situation; in any event they'd lost the house and on top of that there was money owing. They would, therefore, have to look for a flat to rent, Imma would have to go to work, and Carme too. As the meeting ended, Mercè was very upset and said that she wasn't going to let her sister do just anything, but wasn't any more precise than that. There was no way the others, Sebastià aside, could come up with any money to help them out. As a result, it was agreed that the two of them would go and live at Mercè's house and that later on Sebastià would look for a good deal on a flat for them.

'He could look for one for us, too...' my mother let slip while my father was explaining the detail of all this, and he then glared terrifyingly at her, and started hurling insults.

'You fucking bitch!' he yelled at her, right in her face. 'My sister's left a widow and all you're fucking bothered about is yourself!' My mother, frightened and shocked, mumbled that she'd said it without thinking. 'Without thinking...' my father said, glowering at her. 'Don't strain yourself... You're brainless,' he said, rapping her forehead, 'brainless as my fucking bollocks!'

After the accident my father seemed unbalanced, and would kick out at chairs and doors for no reason. That was when I started to think he hated us, had a mania about us, couldn't stand us. For example there was school: for all the indifference I felt about what was said in class, before bed I sometimes mechanically did the homework we'd been given. But when my father saw me sitting myself down at the dining-room table and opening my books, he immediately put the radio on without even looking to see what station it was. I pretended I hadn't noticed, and as I wrote I tried to think about something else. But after a while, he wanted to know if I was going to get on his fucking nerves for long with my homework. I replied that I wasn't, and then he always said the same thing: 'Well get a move on, I want to call it a day...' A moment later he added, to no one in particular, 'Obviously it was never going to be enough having a genius in the house...'

From the kitchen, my mother signalled to me to let it go and, depending how I felt, I either closed my book without having done anything at all, or kept going at my homework as long as I could, still not doing very much, and knowing it could all end badly. And it could all end badly, I worked out, because of Uncle Sebastià, because of the great authority he had over his half-brothers and because he was inaccessible, distant and talked in a different way to them. At least that's what Uncle Pere said when he came to supper shortly after the accident.

'Sebastià,' said my uncle, drawing his head back in the theatrical pose he sometimes adopted, 'really gets on my whatsits big time... Sort of like he knows everyone, never gets it wrong, know what I mean?'

Around then we saw a lot of Uncle Pere because, as I later found out, he had suggested to my father that they start up a business together. It involved renting a warehouse in Poblenou, where they were cheap, and setting it up to buy and sort scrap textile. Wool had one price, cotton another, viscose was worth something else again, and then silk... These offcuts, all mixed up together, could be bought for next to nothing, and then, once it'd all been sorted, they could sell it on at a profit... My father listened very earnestly, childlike, to his brother. Perhaps he just understood that it would liberate him from endlessly unloading lorries and having to put up with that arsehole foreman, as he said almost every day.

It turns out that they had started talking about all this before Uncle Esteve's accident, that they'd consulted Sebastià, who'd told them not to do it, they'd be at each other's throats immediately, and it would all go wrong. That was when Uncle Pere started taking the mickey out of Sebastià, talking about him as disdainfully he could. Obviously the accident complicated things, and it made them fearful. If something like that could happen to Esteve and Carme, who'd had everything easy, what would become of those two, a pair of luckless losers...

When Uncle Esteve was killed in the car, all the talk more or less stopped. My father only saw himself going on for ever with the arsehole foreman and the lorries... That's why he was so wound up, because he didn't know what to do, and hurled at us this blind rage, a rage and violence which seem ridiculous to me now, but back then did a lot of harm. One or two nights I'd heard my father apologising to my mother, whining even, but after three or four days he fell back into his limitless cruelty. Most probably he didn't realise what he was doing, as my mother said to try and excuse him, but bit by bit he built up around him this frightening aura of unpredictability. And it frightened me because when he put out his hand it could just as easily have been to give you a cloying caress as to sink his whole hand into your face. You never knew, and I certainly was petrified of him, so petrified that his presence had become unbearable. Around then I started to remember that, from when I was really quite little, he was forever giving me little smacks on the back of my head. As for my mother, he habitually clouted her on the forehead, telling her she was a dimwit, bugger your cow of a mother and all your bloody relatives... He'd be fine, talking normally, and then all of a sudden he'd turn into a wild animal for no reason at all. What happened next was completely unpredictable: yells, doors slamming, not speaking to us for three or four days at a time... My mother sometimes stroked my hair and said: 'He'll get over it...' but it had always tied my guts up in knots. That and the weather. When the cold started to arrive I was scared of everything: catching a cold, sore throats, leaks, damp... The house was old and the walls were like paper, but at school, which was an enormous building, I also felt that same iciness that started running all over your skin, made your nose itch, and then froze your feet, then your back... When the cold came, there was nothing you could do.

My mother also dreaded the changes in the weather. In winter, going to get water from the fountain was harder work, but then in summer you used more and had to make more trips... In summer, when my father got home he filled a basin full of water and in the middle of the yard, in his underpants, started to wash his face noisily, pouring water over his shoulders and under his arms, soaking himself from top to bottom. He didn't skimp on the water, and when he'd finished, he threw it over the geraniums in the corner.

'Woman...' he'd say, 'more water...' and he'd repeat the whole thing again. It was always like this, his mood changing all the time.

When he wasn't there, things were fine at home; the music on the radio was soft, pleasant and comforting. But then, when he got home, he immediately switched the radio off, saying he had a headache, and asked for aspirin. Then he checked to see if he had a fever, and because he didn't he started to get vindictive. He then told my mother she could put the radio back on, if she liked, never mind he was knackered, the fact that he'd been working like a dog all day didn't matter... My mother said she didn't need the radio on and it was fine as it was.

'I told you to turn it on...' he threatened her. 'Because it'll be my fault if you can't hear that fucking music... You think I don't know what you're like?'

When things were bad, I sometimes went with my mother to the public laundry where she did the washing. It was such a big place, with such high ceilings, and such a strange echo to every sound, that I felt like I'd been set free there. The women shouting, laughing, beating the clothing with a wooden stick before submerging it voluptuously in the soapy water, holding it down with both hands and not bothering if their breasts showed down their fronts... They looked content, happy, liberated, whether they were old and dressed in black, or younger, newly married with their cheeks still fresh and rosy, or the more mature ones who were going through the most difficult stage in their life, as they themselves said. The thing was that when they leaned over the sink to soak the clothes, I couldn't take my eyes off their breasts. And I liked watching, hearing their shrieks and clear, slightly wild laughs, and I liked the way they kept talking as they took the white clothes out of the bluish tinted water. And I also liked the mixed smells of bleach and steamy damp, the sun shining in through the huge open windows...

But sooner or later we had to go home, and then I was scared of the rowing, scared they'd wake me up at midnight and tell me they were sending me off to Menorca, or that they weren't going to let me go out with the gang. I always had thoughts like these, or spent my time looking at the façades of houses, watching people, stopping in front of the photographs the portraitist had put in his shop-window, or talking to Joanet, who also complained about home because his brother was getting worse by the day.

Some afternoons Joanet and I joined up with the lads in the gang and we went on a sort of directionless round trip. We went up Freser Street and stopped at the rag and bone man's. He was a friendly man who let us nose around the shop, which was full of old things. Then we went down Mountain Street, where there were lots of little clothes shops and stores right next to each other. Depending how the mood took them, Ramon and Antonio sometimes rang people's doorbells just to annoy them. Maybe we'd stop for a moment to light a furtive cigarette as well. I was a bit bashful about smoking in the street, but they just went and did it, and more than once Perico had gone up to the first bloke who came along to ask for a light.

Later on we crossed the Meridiana and cut down Clot Street, a street I always found sad, until we got to the market. At that time of day the market was usually half empty. The pots-and-pans sellers who laid out their goods on the ground on big mats had already gone, as had the people selling clothes... Perhaps we'd go as far as the railway station. When we went to the station, which was old and seemed half dead, we sat down to watch the goods trains go by. We liked the way they didn't stop and were long and noisy and how sometimes they made you think they were going to come off the rails and something dreadful would happen.

Perico had just started work in a factory. His father had told him that he didn't need to finish the school year, because so what, the people at work would keep him on the straight and narrow... He went in at six and worked till two in the afternoon. Then, after he'd had his lunch, he settled down for a nap until it was time to meet up with us. He said he didn't like this new job at all, because they made him slave away like a dog, and he had to clean all the machines and mop the floors. Apparently his father wanted him to realise what a chance he'd blown at the watchmaker's.

'The only good thing about that factory place,' said Perico one day, 'is that lots of women work there, so we'll see how it goes...' But he was sad.

Ramon, who was having to help out more and more in the pulse shop all the time, said he was fed up of having to do everything, now school, now the shop, now this, now that... Antonio seemed happy because once the summer was over he'd start work at the ironmonger's, but Salvador on the other hand had to keep studying because he was doing his Higher. The others, Joanet, Miquel and I, being younger, just listened.

'When I'm old enough,' Ramon said now and again, 'I'm going to volunteer for the Air Force. I like the uniform, and

it's a great way of leaving home and never going back...
Flying away...'

If only I could go to work soon, I thought... Joanet said
the same because he was fed up with his mother complaining
and the shit he got from his brother. Miquel on the other
hand said nothing, sometimes getting all shocked when he
heard us telling how Joanet's brother was going around with a
scrubber from the whorehouses – and happily boasting about
it – or when we moaned about the teachers who tried to give
us a hard time with complicated questions about National
Spirit Training...

'What the hell do I know about brotherly love?' said
Ramon.

We talked a lot during these expeditions. Whether Daniel's
father had got ill since he'd been in prison, if it was
pneumonia, about the people at the Ducal cinema place
complaining we didn't go there so often, or that my uncle's
accident had... I remember Perico saying, 'Poor bugger, he'd
only just got that car...'

But I didn't know how to make them see to what extent
this death changed my life. I wasn't able to explain how my
father's and Uncle Pere's plans had ground to a halt and I
couldn't show them the enormous influence Uncle Sebastià's
opinions had at home and the reactions they provoked. There
were things I was ashamed to tell them about, and others that
were just very difficult to understand; for example the endless
subtle links between the kind of life Aunt Lourdes led, and
the afternoon when my father had come home early and my
mother had gone round to a neighbour's house without saying
anything beforehand. When she got back he started shoving
her around as if he was going to throw her out of the house.

'Get out!' he said to her, glassy eyed. 'Get out of here if you like going out so much! Get out and don't come back... Miserable bitch!'

And then when my mother said she'd only been to Maria's house, my father landed one on her which meant she couldn't go anywhere for a few days, more than anything because she was ashamed to go around with her eye puffed up. The boy had done the right thing by dying, I thought. He'd been right to escape from all this torment.

But it wasn't only our house where things were like this. We were all sick of the lives we led. Perhaps Perico didn't know exactly why, but he said he was totally pissed off with living, couldn't give a damn about anything, and would rather have died in the bombing. And Jaume, who hated his father as much as he admired him. Jaume's father, who was very well known in the neighbourhood, worked in a mechanic's workshop, and had been to the gym all his life. He spent some weekends taking part in wrestling matches under the name of The Angel because he went into the ring in a white cape. He went round small towns mostly, although he'd also appeared a couple of times at the Price in Barcelona. They said that despite the name he was as hard as Tarrés and if he got his hands on anyone they were a goner because he could bring them to their knees just by twisting his fingers. Well, this man apparently had some woman, and there were many nights he didn't sleep at home. Jaume's mother had sucked herself dry with crying, but from time to time the man came home full of remorse, saying it was all finished, asking her to forgive him and promising he would never be unfaithful again, but after two or three days it was back to the same...

The only real refuge was the old people's house and the

conversations with César, who always had something new to tell us about. But because Ramon didn't want to go there and the others always went along with him, Joanet and I had to make up reasons to go.

In fact, those very same days, just when Perico had started work and a little after my uncle's accident, the people from the Falangist place said the time had come to sort out the bloke at the watchmaker's. Perico didn't want anything to do with this business and told them it was better to let it rest, that it was all in the past, but they insisted that they'd asked around and the owner of the watchmaker's was a bit suspicious and it would do him good to learn a lesson. So, one night, a group of six or seven Falangists, Ramon, Perico and Jaume went round to the shop, wrote on the walls that he was a red Jewish shit and then stoned the windows.

'It's like they used to do in Germany,' the young man in charge of the Falangists said proudly. According to Jaume it was all really exciting, much more so than the things we normally did in the gang.

They let the watchmaker replace the glass and then when he was least expecting it they stoned it again and daubed paint on the door. They also sent anonymous letters threatening to kick him apart and make him take so many suppositories he'd never stop shitting in his entire fucking life... Another night, to cover their tracks, they broke down a little grocer's door and wrote on the wall that the man didn't have a licence and was selling black market food. Jaume, who was getting more and more caught up in this every day, did it simply for fun, because he had a good time, and when he told us about it he bragged as if he was some kind of big shot.

'I'd give it a rest if I were you...' Perico warned him one day, and Jaume went wild, saying if he hadn't pinched the watch none of this would have happened, and Perico answered that he hadn't stolen anything at all, and he'd better be careful what he said.

'I'll say what I like, okay?' said Jaume, and Perico let it go because he didn't want trouble.

A few weeks later, a man was found beaten up near the swimming pool gardens, with his arms broken, his body all smashed, and we all thought Jaume was involved. He said he wasn't and didn't know anything about it, but it was difficult to believe him because as he listened to us his eyes twinkled and he occasionally let out a laugh.

'Around here,' César explained to us once during one of these afternoon visits Joanet and I made, 'in the war, I saw a house get blown apart by a bomb. I also knew a lad who went into hiding so he wouldn't have to go to the front, and later he was found with a bullet in the back of his head. But the worst was the hunger, the fear and the hunger,' he went on. 'At first, there was the worry that there might be a war. We never really thought that would happen. My parents talked about it, but I never considered it a real possibility. On the day, there were a lot of people at the beach, who had no idea anything unusual was going on. Then there was the whole thing with the anarchists, the violence against the people who'd brought down the Republic. Then the euphoria that the coup had been stopped, because the first battle had been won, as people put it. Later on all the sad news arriving from the front, the ones who came back wounded, the families we knew who'd lost relatives... And then the bombing, and the growing fear people had that there would be no end to it. The radio kept saying everything was going well, but we knew things were going badly and started to get very scared about what the future might bring. At the time, obviously, there were more immediate things to deal with: the bombing, the hunger, the ever-present hunger, which kept us awake at night... People started trying to break into the tobacco and food warehouses... They'd been told there wasn't any, but these places were full... I saw a woman fall into an oil tank and she drowned, just because she wanted, somehow, to get hold of just a little bucketful...'

'What did you do?' Joanet asked.

'Nothing,' he replied. 'What could I do? You couldn't do anything because it was all complete madness. Later on, when the Nationals came into the city, there was a bit more order for a few days, but then all the arrests started, the beatings, and the people who never came home, people who just vanished and no one ever knew what had happened to them...'

'They shot my grandfather,' I said suddenly.

'I know,' said César. 'But don't ever tell anyone. Don't go telling your friend Jaume or those Falange people. It's best to be careful and shut up.'

That's what my mother always said: we should be careful and shut up.

My father and uncle had a lot of doubts before they started the business. Giving up the jobs they held down was scary, as was renting a warehouse that cost them a fortune, although they said it was cheap. Aunt Neli didn't say very much about all of this because the men would sort themselves out, she said, but my mother often remarked to my father that he should think hard about it, because if he didn't have a regular income and things didn't go as planned... Then my father, taking on a superior air which didn't suit him, answered:

'You're always so gloomy about everything... You're like Sebastià...'

At the same time my father and uncle often went to see Aunt Carme, at Mercè's house, and she said the same as Sebastià: they should think very carefully about it because they'd seen how things had turned out for her, and business is all lovely when things go well but if your luck runs out... My aunt had been crushed, drained of all her strength; she held on to my father's hand sometimes and said, 'Such a tragedy...'

All this was making my father anxious, and some days, before supper, I'd see him in the yard with a cigarette in his hand and his head bowed. When I saw him like this I felt the urge to go up to him, put my hand on his arm and tell him not to worry about us, that everything was going to be all right... But I didn't, because I knew that any of this might have shortened his temper and we were the only ones he could yell at... He couldn't do that to his sister Carme, who was ill, and you could see just by looking into her eyes that she carried all the sadness of the world... Nor to Mercè, who would have stood up to him and told him to go fuck himself... And he would have dared even less to say anything to Sebastià, for whom he felt a mixture of respect and envy, as did his brothers and sisters.

My mother was also in a tangle. I heard her say things to a neighbour she occasionally spoke to, and comments she made to Aunt Neli when we ate together... In a way the possibilities of this business had their allure. If things went well perhaps we could rent an apartment, go to Menorca, not be fretting all the time about whether my father'd come up with the weekly money for food and household things... As well as that it would be a slap in the face to my aunts, paying them back for all their graceless comments and the rejection they had subjected her to. It wasn't fair that she was always the one who had difficulties nor that she had to put up with my father going to visit his sisters more than he used to.

'If he wants to see his sisters,' she said to the neighbour 'well, I can understand that, but it's just that he didn't used to go at all, and now it's all the time...'

These things were never discussed at home. In fact nothing was ever discussed at home; there were only arguments, and though I couldn't say why, I saw that beneath the quarrelling lay the tension of things hidden. The father smoking alone in the yard, the mother saying things to the neighbour and the aunt, me not opening my mouth out of fear...

Finally, just when school finished, my father and uncle decided they were going to do what they'd said they would on so many occasions, and just dived in. They were very strange days, which for various reasons I have always remembered, unlike so many other things. School finished the same as every year, but this time the changes were more profound than they appeared, because Ramon, Perico and Antonio started work. In addition to that, Antonio had been dumbfounded by his mother, who was a fat woman, being taken to hospital suddenly after a stroke. She'd always had swollen legs, he said, and according to the doctors it would take time for her to get better, that's if she came through it. Antonio said, 'Women are shit...' But he said this because he, the same as his electrician father, had no idea what to do. 'Now, all we ever eat is omelette...'

During the day it was much hotter than normal for the time of year, and in the middle of the afternoon, there was a sudden, colossal downpour: noisy, huge warm drops that didn't refresh anything. At home, the rain always made my mother very tense, because of the problems with leaks, but actually we hadn't had any for a while because my father had got someone to put a coat of waterproof paint on the roof. It was oppressively close, and this, the damp and the sadness of the rain made me think about my brother. I remembered his death, that great loss which suffocated me for days and days, and I saw his tiny defenceless face. I couldn't cry, I couldn't even admit I was feeling bad, but neither could I help thinking that Joanet and I were now practically alone, and a knot formed in my throat. Since Ramon, Perico and Antonio had started work we saw less of them than before. Salvador also went away to camp for a few days, and before he did he put our backs up when he showed us the knife his parents had bought him, as well as his amazing rucksack. Miquel told Salvador to be careful with the scorpions; he'd heard that where he was going they were huge, and a boy who'd been stung by one had died...

'The poison's horrible,' added Miquel, deadly serious, and Salvador wasn't sure if he was pulling his leg or not.

Around then, the blonde Falangist youth, who was called Ricardo, started to cosy up to Joanet to get him to sign up at their place at the Ducal. But Joanet played hard to get, saying he had too many problems and didn't have the time, and also the few moments he had free he spent with me... One day this Ricardo warned him to be careful who he was friends with, and told him he knew all about my grandfather, and the worst enemies of the Crusade were the communists and the anarchists. Joanet then threw him off the scent a bit, which he knew how to do, and from time to time dropped in, on the pretext of saying hello to Jaume who was still going, more thrilled with it every day. According to him, the place was brilliant; there was a little football table, their own magazine, organised trips, and at certain times of year they went round all the houses with leaflets saying they were going to open the swimming pool in summertime... I couldn't even go near the place. My father would have killed me, more than anything because of his fear that those people would again descend like wolves on the family.

'Those people don't forgive ' my father kept saying, and in this he was in complete agreement with Sebastià, who said, 'Keep well away from the Falange, well away from the police, well away from the military, well away from the priests, and well away from the Civil Guard, although the latter are the most decent...'

'And as for you...' my father warned my mother, 'I've told you before: you talk too much. You say things that'll only bring us trouble...'

'Me?' protested my mother, surprised. 'But I haven't said a word...'

'Well, watch your tongue then, you're prettier when you're silent...' said my father.

Everyone was afraid. My mother and I, my father, Joanet who was scared out of his wits, and then of course there was Daniel, working as a glazier's apprentice now his father was in prison; he had lost a lot of weight and was having stomach aches. But I was most afraid of my father. That uncertainty in his eyes, his unpredictable way of doing things, his harsh way with us, the all-encompassing forceful imposition of his will, the threats, and through all this the solitude he made us endure... I saw it as a huge zone of suffering all around him, an expanse of pain and hurt from which you could not escape. Whatever you did you were always in the same place, you were always wrong, always on your guard, and, always, everything was complicated and difficult.

Naturally all this put more serious with the start of the business. My father appeared unnerved by the project he'd just embarked on, anxious about what would happen if it all went wrong, and the first moments of tension arose with Uncle Pere over little details... However, I had never seen him with so much energy as I did then, and there was even an air of nobility around what he did and why he did it. In the middle of supper one night he said to my mother excitedly, 'If it all goes well, I'll get you a rug so thick that when my sisters walk on it they'll sink in right up to their twats...'

My mother started laughing, saying it didn't have to be as thick as that, and my father replied that we'd see.

One Sunday he took us to see the warehouse. He was tense and when he opened the door to let us in, it was as if he was showing us somewhere luxurious. In fact it was an empty shell, with an asbestos ceiling and wooden beams, unpainted brickwork walls and a cement floor. In one corner was an oldish writing table and some rather small scales.

'They're new,' he said to me, as if he was the child and I the grown-up. 'You want me to weigh you?' And that is the last kind thing I remember about my father, because sure enough, from that day on everything was very hard.

He got up at five in the morning, got on his bicycle and went to work. He and my uncle had bought these bundles of cloth which had to be sorted as quickly as possible. Because of the heat in the warehouse when the sun was up, they went in at dawn, in shorts and T-shirt, and started to separate the cotton, wool, silk, viscose and I don't know what else. After a few days my uncle started getting in a little later and by eight wanted to stop for breakfast. They then went back to the warehouse until lunchtime, spent the afternoons calling on people, going round factory after factory, and two days a week they rented a van from someone they knew in the neighbourhood, delivered what they'd sold and collected what they'd bought.

As the sun went down they returned to the warehouse and sat down on either side of the table and, under a naked bulb, went back to separating out the pieces of cloth according to what they were made of. The place was like an oven, so they left the door open, staying at work until late, until their hearts said enough, and they simply couldn't go on. In the black of night my father came home wiped out, looking like he'd moved heaven and earth, had a bit of supper and went off to his bed with barely a word. But as soon as he was there he immediately called out to my mother.

'Aren't you coming?' he said. That meant I had to go to my room too.

Sometimes, on a Saturday, we went out for the fresh evening air, or had supper at my aunt's. I also seem to remember going to the pictures and variety shows a couple of times, and one night a bolero singer making my mother cry with that song that went: *Those green eyes, their look serene, left in my soul the endless faith of loving...*

On St John's Day, Uncle Pere, with my aunt and cousins, came round for supper and we set up a long table in the yard. My father wore a short-sleeved shirt and we had a good time. He'd spent a lot of money on fireworks, and before we sat down to eat, strolling down the street with the bag of bangers and rockets in his hand, he said with a laugh that he was going to stick a rocket up Sebastià's arse, and then threw bangers at the wall so hard it was as though he wanted to knock it down. This was because things were not going at all badly, despite the difficulties. Both of them made the same wage they were earning before, they paid what had to be paid, and still had a little profit left over.

But bit by bit work was turning into an obsession. At night my father would suddenly wake up, shouting he was going to sort all those bastards out, sweating and pale, his lips completely white. He was left holding on to my mother, helpless, on the verge of tears. My mother stroked him, saying it was all right, telling him to calm down, and gradually she got him to lie back down again and go to sleep. This was upsetting. As if I'd stepped into a forbidden world, consecrated ground that I shouldn't even see, but we lived in a small house and you could hear everything. For example Jaume said he wanked every night before going to sleep, and Joanet often did too, but I didn't dare even touch myself, I never got the chance because I was so scared they'd hear me. I couldn't do anything in the toilet during the day either, because there was no lock on the door. And at night there I was, eyes and ears wide open, and then just as I thought the moment had arrived, my father would turn over with some mumble.

The end of that school year was dreadful because of my father's work, and also because now the other boys were working, Joanet and I had been left all on our own. We didn't like going out with Miquel, who was a real pain with all that sin and hell stuff; we saw little of Salvador, because when he came back from camp his parents imposed a strict study regime on him and he also had to go to French classes with a local lady who worked as a secretary in an office in the city centre. We also only saw Jaume from time to time because he spent hours and hours at the Falangist place...

Joanet and I, though, met up in the mornings after breakfast and went off up Maragall Avenue and beyond, as far as the Guinardó Road, and from there we turned right through the narrow little streets with low houses that took us to the waste ground behind the truck factory. Going from there in a big semicircle, we ended up at the school building, but it was a long walk and we went slowly, so it sometimes took us two or three hours. On the way we stopped to look in the shop windows on the avenue: the mechanic's, the carpenter's, the barber's... I told Joanet how much I loathed the place my father took me to get my hair cut, and as our conversations switched from one thing to another we used to talk about which trade we'd rather learn when the time came to go out to work. We weren't sure. Joanet wondered if he could get a job in a hotel... He liked the whole idea of wearing a uniform, keeping an eye on the doors and taking messages to people's rooms... He only knew about it from the pictures, but it was something he often thought about. I had no clear idea at all. My mother said maybe I could be a mechanic, as there'd always be work in that because there's always machines around, but to me the prospect of going around dirty all the time held no attraction whatsoever. My father hoped I'd go and work with him at the warehouse, sorting cloth. What did I know about the difference between wool and viscose or cotton? I knew nothing about it, but I did know the warehouse made me sad and want to cry.

When Antonio, Perico and Ramon turned up on the street

73

one evening, they started saying that work was a load of shit. You did have more freedom with your parents, you could come and go without having to explain so much, you could say you'd be home late without them asking loads of questions, but on the other hand at work they had you screwed all day, giving you a hard time and buggering you about. The ones who'd been working there for years, the machine operators and technicians, ordered you around a lot because you were only good to be their slave, asking you questions just to make you look stupid... And then the supervisors, who were mostly arseholes, keeping their eye on you and even reporting you to the police if you said anything against the nationalists...

'When they find out who your grandfather was they'll stuff you,' Ramon goaded in his usual provocative way.

Perico told us one day they'd sent him off with a handcart to collect some parts for the machines. They'd loaded it up wrong, and with the problems he had with his leg he couldn't control it and because he was on the Marina bridge, which was quite steep, the cart slipped out of his hands and careered all the way down until it smashed into a kerb and all the parts went all over the place, rolling around everywhere. The passers-by in the street helped him gather them up and an elderly lady on her way to Poblenou offered to go and tell the people at the factory what had happened. After an hour the other apprentices came to help and, having great fun at his expense, they went on and on about what the supervisor's earbashing was going to be like. And, true enough, the row was spectacular. He was a moron, he was totally useless, and one more cock-up like that and he'd be out on the street...

'And you can't just tell them to go fuck themselves, can you?' said Perico when he told us about it. 'You just can't... That's what really fucks you off...'

Antonio told us about how the atmosphere among the apprentices at the ironmonger's was really good fun. There were four of them, and the older ones showed the newer ones all sorts of tricks: when they were sent out to fetch the breakfasts you had to go to one particular bar because there they gave you an extra one for free; the bar-owner's son, who was a woody cretin, always left his cigarette packet hidden under the counter, and you could nick two or three cigarettes a day without him realising. There was one man who worked there who took them to a whorehouse where, although they weren't old enough, they let them in, and according to two lads who'd been, there was one old tart who sucked you off till you came in her mouth...

'Shit, can you imagine what that must be like?' asked Antonio. But neither Joanet nor I could imagine, partly because neither he nor I had been able to make anything come out yet.

We talked a lot about this kind of thing, and what women were like. Whether we went out walking or stayed at Pere's Bar we didn't stop chattering: whether sex was good for your health or if wanking wasn't a sin, that maybe it did make you go weak, or thin, that fuckwit Miquel was far too scared to, and it must be exciting touching a woman down there... We also talked about other things, our parents and how grown-ups' moods changed, about the films we saw and the actresses we liked... All told, that end of term we became very good friends and saw each other every day.

One morning we went to the beach by the sewers, just as

Ramon and the others had shown us. The sun was unbearable, everything smelled of piss, and we were followed by fat green flies that wouldn't stop buzzing around our heads. Joanet was on the point of fainting, and I was acting tough but felt so sick a few times that I nearly threw up. But finally, when we got to the sand, we saw a few people by the water's edge, sunbathing. A couple jumped straight into the sea and dived under, doing the breaststroke; later, from a distance, we saw them waving their arms to us. Joanet and I sat down and passed the time gazing at the women in the wet swimsuits. The breasts of the ones wearing knitted costumes stood out clearly, and you could see the darker area between their legs...

'They say,' said Joanet, 'there are some women who are blonde there.'

'Really?' I said.

'Well, I think so,' he replied. Later on we thought about going on to the shacks, like we'd done with the gang, but in the end we didn't dare.

Joanet's biggest problem really was the story with his brother and mother. The brother, whose name was Manel, didn't sleep at home most of the time, and his mother spent hours on end telling her husband how shameful it was her son had turned out like that, and he ought to be able to make the boy toe the line... The fact of the matter was that Manel was doing it with a hooker, and apparently went to pick her up from work at the same time every day, and she came out happily hugging him, kissing him all over.

'But obviously,' said Joanet, 'during the day this tart's been screwing dozens of blokes...'

With Manel not taking a blind bit of notice at home, and the father having to report to the police all the time, the woman was burned out. She was thin, didn't look well, went out little, and spoke to no one. So Joanet, whenever he could, would take some of his brother's brilliantine, put it in his hair, and get out of the house. It was as if he could breathe all of a sudden, like he could fill his lungs with air, something rarefied and in short supply at home. I told him that for different reasons the same thing happened to me. The only thing my father cared about was his work and he spent the entire day there, so then when he got home he was tired and seemed to have a thing about my mother and me, nothing ever satisfied him, complaining about his brother because he got to work later than him in the morning, and was always so easy-going about everything…

'But the worst thing,' I said to Joanet, telling him about something that had recently happened, 'is that all of a sudden my father decides to paint the walls of the warehouse white, for example, and then there's nothing that's more urgent. He drops everything, gets my mother and me to go with him, makes me spread newspaper all over the floor, then he grabs this big brush and starts rushing around putting this whitewash all over the walls, doesn't stop for breath, yelling at my mother because she hasn't mopped up all the drips properly, and there's all these splashes of paint he's left around the place…

We told each other everything, but at the same time we didn't want to admit that without Ramon, Antonio, Jaume or Perico, we were getting a bit bored. And that's why we sometimes ended up at the old people's house.

We used to go there after lunchtime, when the streets were empty because it was too hot, and one of those afternoons all we could see was Edir, sleeping in the armchair.

We stopped and watched him, and, for sure, with his flies open and the filth on him, he really was a sight. The man, cheeks bright red, was snoring open-mouthed, his hands resting on the arms of the chair. His fingernails were black, as if he'd been carting coal, and between the legs of his trousers you could see a stain that can only have been of piss, and we knew from previous occasions that he gave off a strong and unmistakably sour smell too. When he stood up, it looked like he would just have to fall over, as if there was no way his legs could support him, and he walked unsteadily with one hand on the wall. But that day, Edir was asleep, and didn't notice anything, because unlike when we went there with the gang, Joanet and I hardly made a sound.

After a while watching the curious movements he made with his tongue, as if he was trying to lick his lips, and the tremble of his gigantic fingers, we also saw that his feet were swollen and he wasn't wearing any socks. He had dark scabs with deep yellow rings round them on his ankles. The shirt he was wearing was dirty, and he hadn't shaved for days... After a while we saw the old lady come out running a comb through her hair, and then, when she realised we were in the yard, she told us in Spanish that César had gone out for a walk, and then, looking me in the eye, she said, 'Are you the one who asks questions about books?'

I felt very embarrassed, and for a moment I thought she was accusing me of something. But she sat down on a bench and, still doing her hair, explained to us that she was from Oran, of a Spanish mother and French father, and that when she was little they used to read her books as much in one language as the other. She also remembered the country that she had never been back to, the warm ever-present daytime sun, the expanse of sand and pebble beaches, the strong aroma of spices, the muted colours of walls, the din of the bazaar... When she started reading for herself she was drawn above all to the French novelists. She told us that in those days she liked Balzac, Victor Hugo, Musset, Nerval, Gautier... Nerval, she added, was an example of how Romanticism could combine both the kind with the darkest faces of life... And as if she could read our thoughts, she stopped combing her hair and said to us, 'It's normal that you don't understand me, but keep listening...'

She must have noticed that Joaquet and I were watching her open-mouthed, looking like we were seeing some kind of apparition, since we had no idea what she was talking about, where Oran was, who these people she was talking about were. For César to know things was surprising, but for an old woman to read too... All this meant we felt something between respect and a little fear of Mrs Rosalia, with her sunken eye, and that's why our gaze followed her as she got up, as she put the comb in the pocket of her dress, as she went over to smell the flowers.

'The flowers don't smell like they used to...' she said after a while, and then she asked us what we were thinking about. But as we didn't reply, she went on talking. 'I'm sure you don't know anything about my husband, do you? Well, Gaspar was a journalist, and covered the Tragic Week... He wrote under the name of Pierre, as in Robespierre... But then someone reported him to the police and it all went tits up.'

We could hardly resist the urge to burst out laughing, and, covering our mouths with our hands, did the best we could to hide it. But she continually spoke of incomprehensible, wondrous things. She said *tits*, referred to her husband by his first name, jumbled flowers and books, told us how Mr Gaspar used to work at writing for newspapers... Suddenly, as if she was doing it all for her own benefit, Mrs Rosalia closed her eyes and declaimed, in French: '*Cet amour vague et sans espoir, conçu pour une femme de théâtre, qui tous les soirs me prenait à l'heure du spectacle, pour ne me quitter qu'à l'heure du sommeil, avait son germe dans le souvenir d'Adrienne, fleur de la nuit éclose à la pâle clarté de la lune, fantôme rose et blond glissant sur l'herbe verte à demi baignée de blanches vapeurs...*'

We didn't know what she was saying, but when she had finished these words which meant nothing she turned again to look at us and asked what we were thinking. It was strange how this frail little old woman strolled between flowers and rusty bits of iron, went from looking miles away to coming out with things we didn't understand a single word of...

'The war,' said Joanet in my ear, with the ponderous tone he had when he wanted to be really sensible and get all involved, 'has meant that people who had everything have ended up without so much as a place to die in... But there could be something else here.'

'What are you talking about?' I asked.

'Well,' he said, as if he was thinking about it, 'maybe the whole thing's a lie. I mean, maybe she's made it all up, you know, the old lady. If not, how come, with them knowing so many things, they're even poorer than we are, and we don't know anything?'

That afternoon the relationship we had with the old people changed, and the truth was that both Joanet and I were dying to tell the others in the gang that it wasn't only César who would have a conversation with us and talk about books. The old lady did too. Naturally we didn't think Ramon and the others would believe us. They'd say we'd invented the story about her being from some weird country, because nowadays they went around among adults, and had all this new freedom...

We went round to Ramon's parents' shop and they told us the lad wasn't there, he'd gone out, they didn't know what time he'd be back, most likely wouldn't be in till suppertime, maybe even later... Perico wasn't at home either, nor Antonio, and we preferred not to tell Jaume anything.

Anyway, it seemed to Joanet and me that we had discovered something altogether more interesting. It wasn't that these people were dirty and eccentric, it wasn't just that the giant named Edir had visits from the young woman whose thighs he tried to feel up, nor that César, and in a way the old lady too, treated us differently... More than anything it was that with them the world was wider, it was bigger than just our little neighbourhood, the well on the hill, the hospital, the steep streets we strode up, armed with our flat wooden scooters with two wheels at the back and a bigger one in front, set right between the handlebars... So really, our world wasn't all that bad either... As the seasons came and went, we suddenly found ourselves living in the crazed world of scooters. It was like a fever, and as always was started by Ramon with that long board of his which he'd even put brakes on. Then everyone made one, just about. Jaume was ace at making them, as was Antonio. Perico couldn't go on them, but the rest of us, one way or another, joined in. Salvador had an upright one, and Miquel made a little one that even had a seat, and you could steer it with your feet...

Next, when Joanet and I told each other that craze was over, we entered a phase of setting little traps outside people's houses for them to go and stick their foot in. You made a hole in the ground and filled it with water and dogshit, criss-crossed little twigs over it which you then covered with a bit of newspaper, and last of all you camouflaged it with earth and bits of grass. Or instead we'd seize on a wild idea of going off for miles, or clamber over fences into waste ground, go into factory yards, or scrabble up to the windows at the clinic to spy on the nurses.

We agreed that in spite of the tricks they played on us, the gang of Ramon, Perico, Antonio, Jaume and the others was a good gang. When we were all together, we had even enjoyed assembly in the school playground, in the freezing depth of winter, dressed in vest, shirt, both jumpers, overcoat and scarf, pretending to sing 'Cara al Sol' and there was Antonio, letting off huge farts at each little pause... We always pissed ourselves laughing, and with my arm raised, I could feel my fingertips tingle, and I saw they were blue as if they were about to break off, but I didn't mind...

But all that had ended, and when Joanet and I met up, we spent the hours just roaming around, and he never tired of telling me that our life was shit because our parents were always bad tempered and he explained again that his mother wasn't well and that his father acted as if he wasn't all there... I told him my father seemed a bit crazy, and both my mother and I were afraid of him, but that in a way she was taking the mick as well...

Really, ever since my father went into business with Uncle Pere, everything was complicated. He kept saying that when I was fourteen I'd go and work for him, which terrified me, because if that happened I wouldn't even get the bit of freedom the others talked about. Also, my father was always taking on projects that went wrong. For example, he got it in his head to put up a sign over the warehouse door. Uncle Pere was of the opinion that it was better not to do anything to blow the gaffe on them because they didn't have a licence, but my father appeared not to hear, and had the battens cut for the frame, and also the panel on which he wanted to write something in black letters.

One Sunday morning he made us go down to the warehouse to help him. Actually, I was surprised at the look of the place, which had changed quite a lot since the last time I'd been. It was full of tightly stuffed sacks piled up almost to the ceiling, and to get to some areas you had to walk down a narrow corridor between the stacks. Near the door was what he called the sorter, which was a strange piece of furniture with six legs and a metallic mesh through which the dust and fluff from the offcuts of cloth being graded fell to the floor. The whole warehouse was full of this compacted lumpy dust that stuck to the ceiling, the lightbulbs, the walls, chairs and stools...

'When you come and work here I'll show you all the ins and outs...' said my father in passing and I looked at him without saying anything, but thinking I would find it very difficult to breathe in there. Then, with the door wide open, he started nailing together the battens to make the frame. He worked hurriedly, grumbling constantly, as always. 'Hold that up!' he said to my mother, who took hold of the end of the plank without knowing what she was supposed to do. After a while, as he hammered in very long nails that went all the way through the wood, he screamed, 'Hold it properly, for fuck's sake!'

When he'd finished that, he placed the panel on top, and as we had feared, it was the wrong size for the frame.

'Fucking bollocks...' said my father in a sweat, and my

mother and I felt the urge to laugh, while fearing that would complicate matters more than necessary. Finally, changing the position of the panel, he managed to make it fit on the frame, and hammered it on with smaller nails on all four sides. 'Do you want to nail one in?' he asked, handing me the hammer. And before I could take it from him he added, 'A man's got to know how to hammer in a nail...' I understood perfectly what he said, but pretended I hadn't heard him and started to hammer slowly, afraid I would bend the nail. 'Leave it to me...' he said, grabbing the hammer from me. 'We'll never get it done like that...'

That morning everything went well more or less, and before lunch he'd even managed to paint the wood a pale green which I thought was very ugly. In the afternoon we went back to the warehouse so he could do the letters, which turned out uneven and different sizes. However, it still read 'Pont Bruthers Textil Recycling'. When we got home, my mother whispered to me, so he couldn't hear, 'There's a mistake, isn't there?'

'I think so,' I replied.

And she said, 'Someone else'll tell him when he puts the sign up...'

A few days after he'd put it up, someone duly pointed out that there was an 'e' missing and they had to paint over the whole word to write it again correctly, but no one noticed the mistake with the 'u' which filled me with profound sadness when I looked at it.

In fact, everything to do with that business was painful, and many nights my father sent us to bed early because, he said, he had to do the accounts, and proceeded to cover the table in papers, adding and subtracting amounts until after a while you heard him buggering the whole sodding thing and saying, 'Oi, woman!' and my mother would then get out of bed and go over the calculations. When she found an error and told him, he snatched the paper from her fingers and mumbled 'So where's the mistake?'

'Here,' she said, pointing out that seven plus eight plus two plus three was twenty and not eighteen.

'If you'd been working all day long like I have you wouldn't be so clever at sums...' he muttered. But in the end, when he'd gone over the additions again with his fingers and put a zero where the eight had been, my mother said he had to carry two instead of one, so the next column was wrong as well. 'What, what's wrong with it?' was his only reply, as he turned this simple sum into a torture. I was in my bed, still, eyes closed, feigning sleep, because it was quite possible that he'd make me get up and go over the accounts again.

Some nights though, my father did come home very tired, covered from head to foot in that sticky dust from the warehouse, and my mother prepared a bowl of water for him in the yard and he started washing noisily, in his underpants. I could see the thinness of his legs, and finally, after battling with the water, he raised his head from the bowl and looked at me, hair dripping, and he struck me as a murderer, someone capable of doing anything without a thought.

Joanet was right, our life was shit, and it was basically our parents' fault.

Relations between my father and uncle blew up with the first intense heat of the year. When my mother told the neighbours about it, she said it was a miracle they'd lasted as long as they had, and as usual told more stories than she should:

their personalities were similar, but actually they were quite different in some ways, and her husband had a lot of faults but was a very hard worker, whereas her brother-in-law swanned along through everything, and said Neli was a nag, even if she was her sister, and doubtless goes on at home all the time about your brother this and your brother that... At the same time, my uncle kept doing odd things without even mentioning it, such as for example changing the scales because, as he said afterwards, they were too small... And one day my father exploded and said, screaming, that he'd had enough of all this bollocks and wasn't going to go on doing all this work for other people's benefit, Pere was late every day and took the mickey out of everything he said, couldn't give a fuck whether the walls got painted or not, and then all that stuff with the sign, and the kind of material he was buying in... He couldn't care less about it at all, and that was no way to run a business, because you had to look after a business, focus on the details, not put things off, not think everything'll be all right without putting in the hours, blood sweat and tears, if necessary, because he, my father, said he was prepared to do absolutely anything to keep the family going, which it appeared his brother didn't seem to want to the same degree, or at least he couldn't understand how he could go swanning around like that all the time...

Disaster had been brewing for weeks, perhaps ever since the day they'd started working together, and in that sense it was inevitable. But it was brought about by a series of events, the most serious of which was the deluge of rain that suddenly fell. It was one evening, after a whole day of grey clouds that had rarefied the atmosphere. All of a sudden we heard thunderclaps that rang around in the distance, as if the people in heaven were shifting around huge heavy wardrobes.... Then the clouds dumped all the water in the whole world. At home, the leaks held up pretty well: first there was a patch of damp in my parents' room, then the odd little drip... The yard was like a reservoir, and it was nice in a way to watch the huge brown bubbles the rain produced. Then, though, my father started to say he was beginning to worry about the warehouse, because if the water got in it would bugger up the stock... And so under literally stair-rods of rain, he got his bicycle and went off to the warehouse.

'Wait for it to stop...' my mother told him from under the umbrella as he prepared his bicycle, but he answered, 'You're just like my brother. You can bet your arse he isn't even thinking about it, about the warehouse...'

That night went on for ever. The rain didn't stop and my mother was kept busy now putting a pot by the radio, then a bowl at the foot of the bed. She was anxious because we hadn't heard from my father, and when she told me to go off to bed I felt all tied up in knots, thinking how unfair it was that so much water should fall on us. It was raining on everyone, obviously, but it was more serious for us, because my aunts for example, their houses didn't leak, and other people's businesses weren't at risk either.

At daybreak, when the rain stopped and my father hadn't returned, my mother and I feared the worst. Finally, mid-morning under a blazing sun, my father turned up at home filthy dirty and wild-eyed. He'd spent the night getting water out of the place, where there was indeed a considerable puddle in one corner, luckily only affecting a few sacks. Uncle Pere never showed up, while my father spent hours removing the water and shifting things around. When the rain stopped, he detected the problem was coming from a piece of asbestos tile that was broken. He couldn't fix it on his own, but he'd stayed there to keep an eye on it, as well as to see whether Uncle Pere came or not.

At eight, when my uncle arrived for work, the accusations began. It's no big deal, not that much got wet, stuff the whole bloody thing, you can't run a business like that... They said all kinds of things, yelling and screaming, and then at one point my father gave his brother a shove which very unfortunately made Uncle Pere cut himself slightly on his back against a piece of iron in the wall. That was it. More yells, insults, punches thrown which both of them luckily managed to avoid... My father told his brother they were splitting up, he was leaving the business because he'd rather just work for himself, with no one else, and was going to go and see Sebastià to work out how to go about it... As he explained all this to my mother he periodically smashed his fist down on to the table as if that would solve anything.

'Just when things were starting to get going...' he moaned. Then he added, 'You can't do anything with that arsehole...'

But they couldn't simply abandon the business overnight, and the next day my father decided to go down to the warehouse. He found his brother sitting at the sorting table, working, and discovered he'd had a builder round to fix the leak. But the two of them didn't say a word to each other all day, and just got on with their own stuff.

In the evening, my father washed from head to toe, put on clean clothes and went off to see Sebastià. We never found out what was said at this meeting, but my father came back agitated, not wanting his supper, and after a while he suddenly said he was off to the bar. He'd recently started going to the bar on the corner quite a lot, sitting down to cards with a group of people. He'd come back late, and every time I heard him open the door and close it sharply. Then he'd start making lots of noise, as if he wanted to wake us up: he moved chairs, opened and closed drawers, coughed ferociously as if he needed to spit out his lungs...

They did carry on with the business, but for a long time the two brothers only exchanged the bare minimum of words, and each went his own way, just to screw the other. One would buy stock without telling the other. A truck would arrive out of nowhere and load up I don't know how many kilos of cloth... They had another quarrel, more violent than the last, and this time it was my uncle's turn to say he was going to give the whole thing up. That night my father came home pale, completely colourless, lips trembling. He started yelling at nothing, telling us we were all arseholes, that we'd taken him for an imbecile, that he was fed up with driving himself into the ground for other people... He then started moaning on about what the failure of the business would mean.

'What are we going to live on now?' he shouted at my mother, as if she was responsible for what had happened. When she tried to calm him down, telling him not to worry, that we'd find some solution or other, he always ended up saying the same thing: 'You lot have got it all so easy...'

All this screaming and tension left me disorientated and despondent. I didn't understand the real reasons behind the problem, I didn't know who was right, and when I mentioned it to Joanet, he said as always that life was shit and that adults always made everything complicated.

'Sometimes,' he said to me one day, 'I think the best thing is to get it all over with quickly...' He was pensive, sad, and finally added that he couldn't put up with the yelling and brutality of his brother, who had gone as far as threatening his father... He even said that if he was ever going to kill himself he'd do it just to screw him.

This idea stuck in my head for days and days. While my father went on shouting, when he was sullen and said nothing to us, when he disappeared off to the bar and didn't come back until the small hours, the times he slept at the warehouse because he said he was scared his brother would pinch everything they had... at this time Joanet's idea went through my head: kill yourself, carry out an exemplary act that would leave everyone open-mouthed, beat them with that gesture, because there wasn't anything else I could do.

Naturally I didn't want to kill myself just because of the shouting. It was because all in all it had become unbearable, because that thing about my grandfather, although never mentioned, hovered over us like a mass of guilt... I'd never managed to find out what that man could possibly have done during the war. Sometimes I thought about it and tried to piece together the little fragments I'd heard: the thing about the black car with FAI written on the side, the fact that he had always talked more than he ought to have, the accusation against him that could have come from the grocer, or someone at the market who was jealous, or the boss of the shoeshop... But I never could get to the bottom of it, and was left with the most obvious statements of fact: when the Nationals entered the city they caught up with him immediately and locked him up, in solitary, in Montjuïc Castle, until a few weeks later he was simply shot, just like that, easy as you like. When my grandmother heard the news she lost the power of speech, and was never the same again. They'd taken her Diego, they'd removed her life. Around then, though, a lot of people were killed, and I'd been told that in the mornings they used to find men with a bullet in the head on the beach at Bogatell, and that they took away the dead bodies from the Model prison each night under cover of darkness; Falangists walked into cafés, cast their cold eye over the customers and arrested whoever they wanted to, men, women. According to my mother, the ones you feared the most were the Moors, and then those hypocrite Catalans who so readily jumped to put on the blue shirt and make allegations about people just to feather their own little nest. I would kill myself because of all of this, and because of the sadness that overwhelmed me when the little boy died; and the cold we endured at home through the winters; and the fear my father would hit me when he got angry; and having to stand in the playground every morning and sing with my arm raised... There were many things, because bad things happened one after another to people we knew. One day Antonio got ill, and the doctors said they had to operate immediately or he was done for... It was his appendix and he got through it, but when the gang went to see him in the hospital, he was so thin we hardly recognised him. He wanted to arse around but it took a lot of effort for him to get a smile on his face and say, 'I hope I don't end up with those folk in the other little room...' And we were all well aware what he was talking about, although we didn't say.

Then the man with the white hair, that nightwatchman at the factory, became ill. No one knew what was wrong with him, but he had to give up work, and when he came and sat outside in the fresher air, he looked as if a massive weight had come and knocked him over, leaving him without strength, force or power.

But the worst thing that happened that year was that Daniel's father died in hospital. At first it seemed he was getting over the pneumonia, and because he was feeling better he went back to prison. But after a short time he had a relapse and in a few weeks it was all over. Daniel, who was just skin and bone since his father had been in prison, reacted to the death in a strange way. He seemed to grow up all at once, and as well as working for the glazier, got stuck in to everything he could find. Sometimes, before he went to work in the morning, he delivered newspapers, and helped out at the bakery at the weekends, or at night unloaded crates at a factory. We hardly saw anything of him, but we knew he'd managed to sort it so his mother didn't have to go around cleaning people's houses, and according to my father that lad did nothing but work and work to keep the family going... One day we ran into him at Pere's Bar. He seemed tired, but happy to see us, and he played a game of table football with Miquel. Afterwards he asked after everyone, and when he was leaving he said with sad eyes that he'd drop in to the bar again another day.

Then all of a sudden things seemed to get sorted out a bit at home. One evening we went to supper again at Uncle Pere and Auntie Neli's house. They got on with each other quite normally and there was no mention of the arguments. Aside from all that, my father and uncle were worried about Auntie Carme. Following Uncle Sebastià's suggestion, my aunt had rented a flat near to where Aunt Mercè lived, and turned part of it into a hairdresser's. Aunt Lourdes was helping her with it, and when Aunt Mercè went to see them, she apparently went on endlessly about the years that had gone by with them hardly ever seeing each other. Carme and Lourdes had the knack with women's hair, all the cutting and colouring business, so they weren't doing badly. What's more, Imma – seeing as she spoke English – got a job in an office, but Auntie Carme, who never enjoyed good health, didn't look well and I can't remember ever seeing anyone with such an opaque skin, almost grey...

Uncle Sebastià's skill in solving problems was quite incredible. He did it effortlessly, without getting tangled up in other people's affairs, pointing out the steps he thought it best to take. And, like it or not, you had to admit that since Uncle Esteve's death, Sebastià had managed to overcome the financial holes that had been left, the problems with the banks, the debts... Nobody knew how he'd done it, but they listened to him respectfully, and whatever he said was gospel. So it must have been he who'd made the reconciliation between my father and Uncle Pere possible, in the same way that he'd been able to make use of the tragic events to bring Aunt Lourdes back into the fold of the family and had sorted out so many other things. But we never saw Uncle Sebastià, not that anyone ever moaned, because he lived on a different plane to the rest of us, swathed in everyone's respect and admiration, apart, perhaps, from Uncle Pere, who tended to poke a little mischievous fun.

'Hail he,' said my uncle that time we went to have supper again at their house, 'hail he who lets us have supper...' and, 'he who lets us cut a slice of bread...' and he went on for a good while saying 'he who' each time he made the slightest movement, until my father leant his body over to one side a little, let out a noisy fart and said, 'He who lets me have a shit...' which made all of us laugh.

Joanet and I went to see Antonio quite often after his

operation, because we didn't have anything to do and were getting pretty bored. He spent the day lying in bed, in his underpants, getting as bored as us. He showed us the wound on his belly, a horrible red scar that occasionally made him jump and itched unbearably. But he was all right, seemed happy, and told us again that all this about going out to work was not so marvellous.

'Every day they screw you one way or another,' he explained.

One afternoon there we bumped into Ramon and Perico, and we talked about the others: Daniel, who had almost disappeared off the map; Salvador who spent all day studying like a lunatic because of his father; Miquel, who went through life scared shitless, and Jaume who went round almost exclusively with the Falangist crew. Jaume was as bestial as his father, always full of boasts when we saw him, telling us they'd promised him a job, and when he was old enough he was going to have a gun, he was having a whale of a time, got an afternoon snack every day, did archery, and was learning lots of things that were going to be really useful to him. His father had also joined the Falange because, he told us, these people were very handy for getting wrestling matches at the weekends.

We also talked about the old people, César, Edir, Mr Gaspar and Mrs Rosalia, and we pissed ourselves laughing when we recalled the day the giant somehow hauled himself out of his armchair muttering away like a madman, or evoked in Ramon's words the old lady's rotten teeth and the sour stench her clothes gave off, which was enough to make you faint, or retold the story of Mr Gaspar sitting in the yard, wrapping one of those pencil-thin legs over the other, settling down to meticulously pick his nose.

Joanet and I enjoyed being with the lads and when they started working we came to miss them. Sometimes we even made a nuisance of ourselves going round looking for them. 'He's not here,' someone's mother told us, and one day Perico's father warned us his son was working and not to keep bothering him all the time. This was when we roamed round the neighbourhood talking over our various issues, or we might go down to the beach to see if there were any women in bathing suits. We didn't like girls of our age; they were insipid and dopey, but that summer both Joanet and I had an authentic fascination with grown women.

'When I'm able to go to prostitutes,' Joanet confessed to me one day, 'I'll go for an old tart. I want to see what real women are like... It must be brilliant holding their tits...'

Apparently Perico had been to the Terra Negra, where old women fucked right there at the foot of the mountain, on pieces of cardboard. He'd picked one with very big breasts and, as he explained to us, a soft wet cunt. At night I could not get this idea out of my head, and I also thought about the thighs of a neighbour I'd caught a glimpse of when she sat out in the evening, generous, white thighs, or the women at the laundry leaning forward to soak the washing, revealing massive cleavages, deep and swaying... I'd learned to masturbate slowly, not making any noise, with my legs tensed and my eyes wide open, until I couldn't catch my breath. Afterwards I always looked to see if anything had come out.

When he'd recovered from the operation, Antonio also decided to do it with a whore, even though he wasn't old enough. Perico's story had got him going just like the rest of us, but he said he wanted to try and get into a brothel and shag a tart in a bed. He had an address, and when he told us all about it afterwards he seemed satisfied. This woman was also older, older than his mother, and according to Antonio, as soon as she'd got the money she took her clothes off and washed him in the basin, standing up. After she'd touched it for a while, when she saw he was ready, she said to him, 'Put it in me,' and Antonio then started moving like he was losing his brains, having this really intense feeling, he said. Once he'd finished, she slapped him playfully on his bum and told him to take it out. 'It's your first time, isn't it?' the woman said afterwards, to which he replied that it was. 'Well, now you know dearie, you come back whenever you like...'

For days and days we did nothing but talk about this, and for a spell Joanet and I both masturbated every day. One afternoon we even did so together, up on the mountain, behind some thickets where we knew no one went. We sat opposite each other and ended up bruising ourselves, because we kept going and going until we couldn't any more.

'Jesus Christ, God how I wish I could come,' said Joanet, who had a long, thin dick.

Some days, Joanet and I went to the old people's house earlier than usual. First we looked through the door on the lane that gave on to the yard, an old door full of holes and splits. We could see the white dog and the cats lying in the yard, or Edir, coming slowly down the corridor from the toilet with one hand on the wall, or maybe old Mrs Rosalia watering the plants... We knew César wasn't in at that time of day and that Mr Gaspar was still in bed. He used to get up around midday, always in a bad mood, and when he went out to the yard he already had on that double-breasted jacket which must have been baking hot, his cigarette in his mouth...

We liked snooping, and whatever these people did we

found bizarre, even the most trivial things, so we spent a lot of time peeking through the front door, making nervous little jokes. Finally, when Mrs Rosalia noticed, she shrieked, as if we'd surprised her, and said to us gruffly, 'What is it? What do you want?' but then went on pottering round the yard, and after no time at all she was talking to us about all those things we enjoyed so much. 'When my daughter lived here, this garden was quite another place. We had a big wicker armchair where I used to sit and read, but then of course we had a fight over it, because when she got married she took it away with her... It was very comfortable. The cats liked it too...' she said, laughing in such a way that she displayed her mangled gums. 'At night,' she went on later, as if she was talking about something else, 'I used to sit and watch the stars. Do you like looking at the heavens? You ought to try it. You can learn a lot, you realise how insignificant we are. Do you know what I mean?'

We said yes, more than anything just so she'd continue talking, and she then explained what the Milky Way was like and where the North Star was, adding that the Chinese liked looking at the stars, they were a cultured people, and we westerners were small fry next to those people we never even thought about, as if they didn't exist...

'The day the Chinese arise from their slumbers,' she said to us once, very seriously, as if she wanted to frighten us, 'we might as well panic... They'll annihilate us, no doubt about it... Our world won't be able to withstand the force of the wise cruel orientals. You mark my words... In their culture they've maintained a splendid mix of refinement and savage primitivism. Any society which knew how to establish the concept of the efficient civil servant has to make you think...

You've heard of mandarins, haven't you? Well, there you have it... And as for gods, they understand gods quite differently... We say they're all under the influence of opium, but like Sybils we keep quiet about the fact we westerners induced them to it... Those blonde giants in iron ships...'

Naturally we didn't know what she was talking about, but we sat by her and listened spellbound, until she said she had work to do and got up. Sometimes Joanet and I stayed a little longer, playing with the dog, who knew us and let us stroke him. One day Edir made guttural noises and smiled as he showed us the centre spread of a newspaper.

'What's he saying?' said Joanet.

'I don't know...' I replied, and as we approached the giant he mumbled, 'It's all going down the pan...'

We always left the house in a state of fascination, our heads full of fantastic images all jumbled together in a delirious mix: stars, gods, the Chinese, mandarins, opium, the giant... We didn't know what mandarins or opium were, and we didn't know what Edir was trying to tell us either, but we realised that these people weren't crazy, which is what people said around the neighbourhood, and we thought it was unfair that Mrs Rosalia was seen as little more than a witch.

Afterwards, if it was the afternoon, we'd drop in to the bar to see if anyone was around. Sometimes Jaume was there, at the bar, doing nothing. When he saw us he put on a smile and gave us a hug. He wanted to know what we were up to, how the summer was going, why we didn't go round the swimming pool... We never spoke to him about the old people, nor what we thought about women. We'd got a little bit frightened of Jaume, especially since he'd been going around the streets in the blue shirt uniform, telling everyone the Falange had been created to save Spain and turn it into an empire.

'Spain,' he said, repeating everything he'd been taught, 'is an Indivisible Unity, and must recover the greatness of when the Catholic Kings saved us from the Moors. It's to achieve this that we must serve her and always take the path that leads through the stars.'

'That leads where?' Perico asked him one day.

'Through the stars,' repeated Jaume. 'And that means we can't tell lies, we have to be happy and behave in a manly way. No poofs. You've got to be with the workers, that's why we wear this shirt, and the black tie means we're in perpetual mourning for José Antonio. You know how it is when someone dies, people wear black armbands? Well, you see, we wear the tie.'

He went on to explain that he was a supporter, and that within five years he would become an activist. My mother warned me several times not to go around with him, to watch out and, reminding me all about my grandfather, she explained that these people offered lots of things to lure kids in, and then made them tell them what everyone said at home, if people were saying things against the people who made the rules, if they had compromising documents, or were hiding someone. It was all a lie, according to my mother, and people like us had to watch out.

'Just look at Daniel's father: he was a good man... If your father knew you went around with that boy...' she said to me.

But that summer my father was oblivious to everything; all he thought about was the warehouse, and at home virtually the only time he ever opened his mouth was to be abusive. He looked tired, always with that very fine dust in his hair, and dirty fingernails... When he sat down at the table, he closed his eyes and started to eat without a word, making more noise than ever slurping his spoon. He liked doing that, just as he liked putting black pepper in his soup or a glug of wine in the plain boiled rice, all the time grumpy. He then got a stomach ache and had half a glass of water with bicarbonate and immediately let out a dreadful belch. Finally, before he'd quite finished chewing, he lit a cigarette, filled his lungs deep full of smoke and exhaled it slowly, as if that would calm him down and he would find a little peace. But just a moment later he said, 'You know what he's gone and done today, that brother-in-law of yours?' addressing himself to my mother. 'It looks like that lad really enjoys getting on my tits,' he went on, after a pause accusing my mother, 'are you listening to me or not?'

'Of course I'm listening to you,' she said.

'That lad...' he continued, referring to my uncle like that, 'for him it's not enough to get to work late, and spend hours over his breakfast... He's got a new one now. Instead of having lunch, he goes and has a kip on the sacks and then in the middle of the afternoon he eats the sandwich your sister's made for him. Eat,' he said menacingly to me, stabbing a glare at me as if I was the one who was having the kip. 'And of course,' he continued, 'the miserable fucker who's sweating his bollocks off all day is me. He's perfectly happy just taking his wages... What do you make of that?'

'You know what he's like...' said my mother, and he immediately leapt up.

'So it seems that it's only him who's allowed to be special, is it? We'd be in a fine state if I went around kipping all day too... Good thing I've got something going and soon I'll be able to tell him to go fuck himself, and we'll have dosh coming out our ears...'

During these suppers I felt like crying. In some respects I felt grown up, even more grown up than I was, and felt I had it in me to go out to work, but sometimes with my father it was as if he made me so small, as though the way he was wouldn't allow me to grow up. My mother too was petrified when she saw him like this. And it was as if he had a need to feel that people were scared of him, as if he needed to beat down everyone else so he could flourish a little in that small suffocating house.

'There was another bastard today with a death wish...' he continued. 'He thinks I'm a sucker. He thought he could cheat me on some worsted for more than the real price... I told him to go fuck himself. One of these days I'll crush these people like beetles, I'll listen to them fart under my foot, and then I'll shit on the white gunge that's left of them...'

'Don't get like that...' said my mother as she went into the kitchen.

'I'll get any damned way I fancy...' he concluded.

All I wanted to do was go to my bed, but I couldn't do that until he said it was time to, or he went off to the bar. I felt better in bed, although I kept moving from fear of my father to the powerful hate building in me of this man who without any justification made us suffer. Then I was suddenly carried away by a sea of desire, a burning desire making me think, eyes closed, about having a woman, touching all women, letting them slowly wash me, hearing them ask me to penetrate them, empty myself into them... The others, apart from Joanet and me, could all come. It won't be long, I told myself, it won't be long...

Later on I thought about my aunts, my cousin Imma, who had very black hair and was tall, with big eyes. And I thought about the old people, and the books I'd heard them talking about but didn't dare ask them for, like the one about a boy who enlists on a ship, and in the end is lost in the cold fog, in a white sea ever more dense and calm, almost frozen, at the South Pole...

My mind wandered. Maybe living on the island with the relatives would have been better, not hearing all the shouting, not seeing any of the people I knew, not having to go and work with my father... Perhaps one day I would be still, not breathing, until I went to sleep for ever... Maybe the summer would be over soon, and in autumn it would start to rain for ever, the house would be flooded and we would all drown... Perhaps time would stop and I would never have to wake again, feeling the gentle tickling in my eyes, on the point of sleep, stroking myself, waiting to grow up... And soon I did, of course.

Dog Days

And autumn arrived, a wild autumn full of obstacles. The first few days the wind shook the leaves off the trees, brought them to the ground and dragged them through the streets, and then it started to rain.

My father was more tense by the day, and after supper, while he was in the bar, my mother and I sat listening to the radio. She sewed, I opened my schoolbooks and looked over them without enthusiasm. One night, before my father got back, my mother said to me without lifting her head from the shirt she was repairing that in the spring there was going to be one more at home, that I would have a little brother, or a little sister. I felt great embarrassment, and then I realised she had tears in her eyes.

'Do you mind?' she asked me.

'No,' I said, but immediately into my head came the poor child who had died and I was terrified of going through something like that again. And as if she could read my thoughts, she added, 'This time everything'll be all right.'

Naturally I told Joanet the next day and his response was very clear.

'Shit,' he said, 'And you're going to have to look after it...'

'No, I'm going out to work.'

We hadn't talked at all about this subject, but because of my age, and the question of money, all in all it was clear that this would be my last year at school. I didn't mind giving up the ghastly sad building where I wasted hours for nothing, but I remember thinking that before I left school I had to get closer to the world of Mrs Rosalia, César, and books. 'I must read,' I urged myself, 'I must always read. My salvation will be books.'

And so before the school term began I went to the old people's house more often than normal. Generally I went with Joanet, and we spent the time talking with César, who had hurt his foot and couldn't work. Those days he spoke to us of an incredible story that had us captivated. It was the life of a man who after two shipwrecks and being kidnapped by pirates ends up alone on an island with nothing more than the bits and pieces he can salvage from the ship. He builds himself a house up in the trees, plants things to eat, hunts, goes looking round the island...

'Robinson,' according to what César told us, 'is the spirit of an era, but at the same time is the deep solitude in which we humans live; it's the learning of the simplest things, the value of effort and friendship, and the differences that exist between people... But it never ceases to be a wonderful adventure story.'

Suddenly, without a second thought, I asked him if he would lend me this book he was telling us about. He replied that yes he would and went into the house to fetch it. I remember that after a moment he brought it to me in both hands and I received it like that too, respectful. It was a thick book, and I feared I might not have it in me to read it, but on the cover it said in big red letters: 'Robinson Crusoe', and at the top the name of the person who had written it, Daniel Defoe.

This opened up to me a new world and that week instead of going out with Joanet I stayed at home, reading. It was the first time I had held a book that wasn't a school one, and also the first time I'd read for pleasure. At first I found it difficult, and I had to go back over the previous lines, but soon I entered into the life and adventures of this hapless man. *'Nothing can describe the confusion of thought which I felt when I sank into the water; for though I swam very well, yet I could not deliver myself from the waves so as to draw breath...'*

This was what was happening to me, I told myself. I also had the sensation that enormous waves were submerging me in a deep sea... I had to struggle against this force that sometimes sucked me into the darkness or pushed me toward an uncertain destiny. My life too was full of difficulties, of doubts, hopes and errors.

Joanet came looking for me a few times. The first time I said I couldn't come out, that I'd been grounded, and he believed me. The second time I said the same thing but he looked at me quizzically and wanted to know what was going on.

'Nothing,' I replied, 'You know how it is, with my father and everything...'

He believed this too, but the third time he could see I was deceiving him and I had to tell him the truth. I was reading that book of César's and wanted to finish it as quickly as possible, before we went back to school. Robinson's life was drawing me along; I'd never experienced an emotion like it, and I just couldn't put the book down at all. Every page was better than the one before, and as I went on reading I learned to know this man who was so like me... I had never been to Brazil, I couldn't swim like him, I'd never known the hardship of the privateers, but in a certain way we were identical, and this similarity filled me with pride. Sometimes I would sit on my bed and with two pillows behind my back he and I roamed the island. '*I now resolved to travel quite across to the sea-shore on that side; so, taking my gun, a hatchet, and my dog, and a larger quantity of powder and shot than usual, with two biscuit-cakes and a great bunch of raisins in my pouch for my store, I began my journey.*' I was sorry I hadn't gone to the island; who knows whether somewhere else, far from the city, some of these adventures might have been possible... And I imagined myself with a pouch on my back, leaving a little cove, climbing up between the bushes and the burning rocks, hearing the cicadas, feeling the sun on my face...

When I got tired of lying on my bed I sat myself down by the window and continued reading. At night, before my father got back from the bar, I also read, and when the book gave me a moment of great pleasure I would sometimes stop for a moment, look at the jacket, run my fingers over the name of the author and then put my hand warmly on the cover with my eyes closed as if by doing this I might manage to absorb the contents of the pages without having to run my eyes over them. '*This was the pleasantest year of all the life I led in this place. Friday began to talk pretty well, and understand the names of almost everything I had occasion to call for...*' He would learn things about me, and I would learn from him... We would have to fight the cannibals... I'd have a dog... I didn't understand how Robinson treated so badly the savage who had saved his life... Sometimes I felt a lump in my throat which almost made me cry and then filled me with tenderness.

As I read I also realised things I had never thought about until then: how difficult it was to build a house, that any little object could have a use, that you had to make a constant effort to survive... And as I continued, my head increasingly went off onto one thing then another. I thought about myself, the deep sensation of abandonment I felt at school, the fear of the new developments that had been announced, my father's character, always so difficult... But above all I was swept along by the vicissitudes, the toils and hopes of poor Robinson, and then I forgot about the stormy days of the end of September and the child who was to come. In fact my mother thought it was odd that I spent the days with this book in my hands.

'Is that from school?' she asked me on one occasion. I replied that it wasn't. 'Don't let it distract you from your obligations...' she said.

I didn't know what obligations she was referring to. In actual fact I didn't have anything to do until school started. Sometimes I went to fetch in the bread, or my mother sent me to Mr Lluis's shop to get rice, noodles, potatoes... It was always the same. I read out the little list I had and Mr Lluis, who looked like he'd dyed his moustache and hair, put it all in the basket for me. Then I had to say the most difficult bit, that my mother would come in on Saturday afternoon to pay, and at that point Mr Lluis, very serious, opened up a notebook where he wrote down what people owed him. In the back of the shop his wife, who was fat, spent her time picking up stitches in stockings with a little machine that buzzed occasionally and made my ears tickle. That was all I had to do. Those were my obligations.

When I finally finished the book, and with barely a thought, I started again from the beginning: '*I was born in the year 1632, in the city of York, of a good family...*' I had a desire to relive it all, wanted the images of the island to be engraved in my memory for ever. I was convinced I would never again find anything better. And in fact this second time everything was clearer to me, more intense and enjoyable than before.

All the same I did go out with Joanet the odd time. I explained to him what I had experienced with the book; we went round the streets once again, dropped into the football bar to see if anyone was there... Perico spent quite a lot of time there. He had changed, seemed older, and had tried to grow a little pencil moustache that made us piss ourselves laughing. He told us they wanted to operate on his leg to see if like that it would give him less trouble, but the doctor wasn't at all clear and said it might end up rigid, all solid.

'These butchers are arseholes... But seeing as it always hurts so much...'

One day I went to give the book back to César. I went there on my own, one rainy afternoon, and to keep it from getting wet I wrapped it in three sheets of newspaper. It was the first time I had been inside the old people's house. Up to then we had always been in the yard, and although we could see the interior from outside, I had never imagined that they lived like this. After the first area, which was where the kitchen was and Edir sat, there was a square table on the right with a corner bench seat and two chairs, and on the left César had his bunk where he slept. He didn't call it a bunk, but I always liked the word because my father used to use it, especially when he wanted to go to the cinema and my mother would ask what was on; he always answered the same way.

'*Pursued to the Bunk,*' he'd say, 'And then part two, which is called *The Burning Bunk.*'

Anyway, next to his bunk César had shelves full of books. There were lots of them, but you could hardly see their titles because the room was dark, and as they didn't have electricity and used oil lamps you had to take the yellow flame right up to the spines to see them. The first day this very simple action of taking the oil lamp fascinated me because, by transporting it, César made the shadows move, especially his own, which suddenly lengthened on the wall, ghost-like and sinister. The smallest shift made the entire room change. If the movements were slow, spectres began circulating unhurriedly, and if he changed direction rapidly, the room shook to the point of disfigurement. There was a moment when I could clearly see César's yellowed face and two faint silhouettes projected behind him, but I wasn't afraid. Everything that happened in that house was special, different, bizarre, but you had to take it as it was.

'If you like, I'll lend you another one...' said César, offering me a book. 'Here, read *A Journal of the Plague Year*.' I took it, although I was afraid that with school I wasn't going to have time to read it as quickly. I told him this, and he replied: 'If you open it, you're done for... You won't be able to put it down.'

But I didn't open it until long afterwards, because before going back to school my father and Uncle Pere's great row blew up. One night, at suppertime, my uncle burst in through the door. He was angry and started asking my father to explain about some things he had bought.

'Don't you go and get me involved...' he said excitedly,

threatening him with his finger. 'Or maybe you want them to throw us in the slammer?'

My father, who was eating, was taken aback, his face all pale, but he simply said that no one was going to throw him in the slammer. It seemed that the roles had literally been reversed. My uncle put his hands down furiously on the table and approached my father to speak to him, and my father in contrast was smiling, joking, telling him to calm down. My mother was frightened and asked them not to fight, and my uncle answered her, 'Can't you see, this moron is going to lead you into rack and ruin...?'

Neither my mother nor I knew what they were talking about, but later on I worked out that my father had bought a truckful of offcuts that had been stolen from some factory. It appeared this wasn't the first time he'd done this, but seeing as my uncle hadn't wanted anything to do with it, my father closed the deals all on his own and organised everything so that the sacks went directly to the person who was buying them. This time, because of a mistake on the part of the haulier, the sacks had been unloaded at the warehouse and my uncle had immediately seen trouble looming.

'Come on mate, everybody does it...' argued my father after a while, not even getting up. And he then added: 'If you don't want to earn yourself a living, maybe you'd be better off on your own.' My uncle started yelling then, and my father stood up, his face white and his lips bloodless. 'Don't yell,' he warned him in a barely audible voice, but it was as though my uncle had lost his senses and just went on accusing him of things. He thumped his hands against the wall saying he couldn't work with someone who was always changing his mind, he was sick of all the petty obsessions, always getting those black looks from him as if he was lucky to be alive, fed up with hearing stupid remarks and getting caught up in cock and bull stories that only succeeded in pissing people off.

'It's all very well painting signs,' he said, 'all very well showing off in the bar about how well everything's going, and then you go and land yourself in the shit. You're a big-mouthed prat. You're a joke.'

My father lunged at him and my uncle accidentally broke a pane of glass in the door with his elbow. I didn't know what to do, I was next to my mother who was crying, begging them not to fight. Large tears fell down her cheeks and at one point she put her hands over her face, and with a lump in my throat I sensed my legs giving way. It was only for a second, maybe less, but I felt my mother take hold of me under my arm. To me this was all humiliation, this scene, losing my grip on things, being powerless to do anything... Next I heard a loud violent slam of the door, my uncle repeating as he left about him being a big-mouthed feckless idiotic prat...

From that day on it wasn't possible to talk about my uncle at home, nor about Aunt Neli or my cousins. My mother couldn't go and see her sister either, and once again Uncle Sebastià had to intervene to sort out the money matters.

And it was determined that my father would end up with the warehouse and a small part of the stock. Every day, crazed as he was, he left the house at five in the morning to go to work on his bicycle. He sat and sorted, hardly ate, got thin, and in the evenings came home late, dirtier and more bad-tempered than ever. There were weeks when we hardly ever saw him. He turned into noises I learned to recognise from my bed: the cough in the morning, when he got up, the muttering when he ate in the evening, the farts he let off when he went to bed... He even worked Sundays, never stopped, and one day when Aunt Neli came round secretly, I heard my mother tell her that recently he'd been giving her a bit more money and everything was going well, except that he was killing himself with work.

'Seeing as he's never around, I'm calmer but I don't know how all this is going to turn out...'

'Badly,' said my aunt. 'As always...'

Now I'd started back at school I spent my days doing nothing, possibly even more bored than before. In class the other kids talked, drew, wrote, but I don't remember ever writing anything, or going up to the blackboard, or ever opening a book. Obviously I did do so, but it has been completely wiped from my memory. In fact there are very few things I do remember from school: I remember being given a fountain pen, and the year we started using ink. School had become this leaden place where the hours never quite went by. Inside the classroom there was always this faint whitish cloud, as if the fine dust that the teacher's chalk created spread itself over our heads and then fell bit by bit, imperceptibly, to deposit itself on our hair, our clothes, our shoes, and then the floor...

Out of the window all I could see was grey sky, overcast and dead. The teacher was dressed in black and always wore a tie. This year it was a short man with little legs, baldish and with a round face that spoke a strange kind of Spanish to us, addressing us formally. He ascended to the dais with a certain amount of difficulty, turned his head to us, looked at us, and said things such as: 'This morning, class, you will endeavour to understand basic notions of history which will doubtless be of use to you in the future...'

This voice reached me from far away and was like an echo approaching slowly, winding its way, then surrounding me sparingly, finally brushing the back of my neck like a dreadful frozen hand, ultimately losing itself in the chilly depths of the classroom, in a remote corner where it reverberated almost inaudibly and quite mysteriously for hours and hours.

But if I was drawn to anything it was the greeny brightness of the rain through the windows. One or two mornings I thought I saw the golden reflection of sun on the glass. At other times it was instead even darker than usual and beyond the window all I could make out was watery blackness, as though the whole classroom had been submerged in a depthless silent ocean I was sure we would never emerge from again.

Eventually the lights were turned on and the four yellow globes hanging from the ceiling were distant and useless. I looked at them by raising only my eyes, not moving my head. I was convinced that one day or another these globes would fall and cause a horrendous explosion. Or they would suddenly be extinguished and we would have to stay still for ever more, sitting at our desks in the dark, guessing at the movements of the others, feeling the cold enter gradually up our sleeves, rising up our trouser legs, then crawling like a little snake up to our hair, our necks, the collar of our shirts, to end up tumbling down our backs. It also passed through our clothes to grab hold of our bones so tightly that I was convinced we'd never be able to budge an inch again...

There was nothing worse than the defencelessness I felt at school those lightless days, those interminable winter days, subjugated by an infinite solitude that, all the same, welcomed me into a sadness which was not only mine. The classroom, the whole school, was gripped by the cold which at going home time spilled out through the equally lightless streets, turning itself into black, grotesque faces in doorways, shining foully at windows, spreading out a little at the empty shops and the icy dead bars. At that point I'd only been to a few places around the city, but I imagined it all dark and dirty, crisscrossed by trams jangling and rumbling along the tracks, inhabited only by the ghosts of those who hadn't survived the worst years.

Perico had the operation, and with the excuse of going to see him, the gang met up again. It was the same as all the other times: Antonio said the ironmonger's was a pile of shit and that he spent all day going up and down ladders just to sell half a dozen screws, a plank of wood, a few nails, a hammer... Ramon said he was fine at his parents' shop, they let him get on with things, didn't ask loads of questions and he could come and go as he pleased... He was still obsessed with becoming an aviator, and apparently he'd even been to find out what you had to do to get into it. We hardly ever saw Salvador. By this time he was going to the same school as Joanet and me but in a different class, with lads doing the higher certificate. They told me I didn't look well, and wanted to know if I was wanking too much. I replied that I was tired and that was all, but in truth those were the worst days of my life.

At home everything was all the same as well: the noises that reached me from the dining room when my father got home at night, me curling up in bed and closing my eyes, the sharp bang when he closed a drawer, the little explosion when he took the top off the fizzy lemon bottle... It seemed to me that I could hear him chew, hear him break a piece of bread off the loaf, hear him gulp down the cold potatoes... The

Sundays he didn't work he spent in bed, sleeping, and got up mid-afternoon, with two or three days' stubble on him, hair all over the place, asking for his lunch. Sometimes he looked at me as if he hated me, and he treated my mother badly too. Later he'd go off to the bar and come back when we were already in bed, feigning sleep.

What frightened me most was when one day my father said I'd have to leave school and go and work with him. I imagined myself lost among rows of stuffed-full sacks, or sitting at the sorting table spending hour after hour going through dusty bits of cloth... with my father always looking at me in that strange way, occasionally giving me a cuff on the head, making fun of me at breakfast in the bar, in front of all the other men there... If he made me go there, I told myself, I'd leave home, get away, start walking and never turn back... All day and all night, I did nothing other than go over and over this dreadful idea, which to my thinking made school into a lesser evil, a refuge, a place of boredom but where nevertheless nobody bothered me. But as my father got more and more work I saw the fateful day fast approaching when he would say that was enough of me wasting my time, I'd better pull my finger out, I had to earn a living, I had to go and work for him, that way I'd learn what graft was all about, enough of all that loafing around...

With all this, I didn't dare open the book César had lent me. I felt that as soon as I did my father would come in, take it from my hands and throw it out with the rubbish. When I went out in the afternoon I didn't think about reading either. Joanet and I were miserable. He said he wanted to go out to work right away, that school was a complete waste of time. I was more than ever crushed by fear, sadness and bewilderment.

Sometimes I was able to identify these thoughts with great clarity, and even managed to work out their origins: I was frightened of my father's behaviour, scared of how he'd react, petrified he'd hit me or give me that fevered look... Having to have a brother made me sad, isolated me from the others, deepened my loneliness. And I didn't know why I went to school, or what I'd end up doing in a few years' time, found it hard to see myself spending all my time at the warehouse, having to endlessly plough through dirty scraps of cloth...

The worst moments came at night, when I closed my eyes and lay still, unable to sleep, on guard for each mutter or sigh. Then shoes falling to the floor would make me shudder, the creak of a wardrobe door caused me anguish, the little bit of light coming in through the window made me fear it was already morning... In addition, I'd got over the craze of masturbation. I didn't want to do anything, all I wanted was for time to be wiped away, that it would just stop, that nothing more would happen in my life... When we got out of school in the afternoons, Joanet and I sometimes hung around the football bar, watching the people coming and going on the street, realising each day it was getting dark earlier, telling each other we already needed jumpers, and I didn't tell him, but I felt that our life was absurd and pointless.

'You're worse than I am...' he told me, looking at me.

One day I took the book about the plague to school and as the teacher went on talking about whatever, I placed it on top of the desk. I opened it carefully so no one could see me and I was immediately captivated by how Defoe described the outbreak of the disease. But I was reluctant to go on, not wanting the teacher to catch me reading books that weren't to do with class, so I closed it, knowing intuitively that when I was able to read it I would discover a gruesome world. In fact I learned the first few lines by heart, and both at school and at home I would frequently recite them to myself, eyes closed. '*It was about the beginning of September, 1664, that I, among the rest of my neighbours, heard in ordinary discourse that the plague was returned again in Holland...*' I don't know what it was about the start of the book that I found so extraordinary. I didn't understand it, but I felt that very quickly and clearly he painted a scene, a situation, and a threat. In any case, I lived for days with this consoling hope. I had another book to read, and wasn't entirely alone. At supper, at school, walking down the street, if that opening came into my head, I greeted it with a mixture of joy and unease; it was like being told a secret: '*It was about the beginning of September, 1664, that I, among the rest of my neighbours, heard in ordinary discourse that the plague was returned again in Holland...*'

That autumn, Aunt Mercè and her husband bought themselves a Traveller, a car with wooden bodywork. Oddly, they wanted us to go and see it, and told us that Sebastià was going to be there as well. It was always delicate going to see my aunt; my father, sure we'd bump into Uncle Pere if he went, decided we weren't going, and sent my mother to pass on the message. But my mother came back saying that, according to Mercè, Sebastià wanted all of us there, that there was a problem with the family, and we had to talk. As far as I knew there had never been a meeting like this, and my father had a dreadful few days of it, because on the one hand he didn't want to come across my uncle, even less so in front of the rest of them, but he didn't dare disobey Sebastià either. So that week was all tempers, grim faces and yells. One day my mother said to one of the neighbours that she couldn't stand it any more, couldn't breathe air, her legs were always shaking, and sometimes she wet herself...

'Well it won't do you any good getting upset right now...' said the neighbour, and my mother just looked at her not knowing what to say.

But my father seemed oblivious to everything. In his character there was something wild and invincible, but at the same time he seemed trapped, defenceless, furious and blinded by his obsession with imposing his authority on those of us around him.

Anything at all could be enough for him to reprimand, throw a chair at the wall, slam a door or come out with insults. He often told my mother she was a waste of space, a heap of shit, that without him she'd just go starve, and as for me he'd stick a huge thick menacing finger right in front of my eyes and tell me he didn't want any layabouts in his house, warning me without saying it that soon I'd have to go and work for him at the warehouse and you can forget about all those books. 'I'll kill myself,' I thought at that moment, and especially so when I saw my face in the mirror when I was washing and realised he and I looked like each other in a way: the same pale eyes, the same thin lips... Right then I wanted to cry. I splashed water over my face so my mother wouldn't notice and went off to school with a lump in my throat. Naturally neither he, nor I, nor my mother knew to what extent it was unreasonable and unnecessary to live like this. Sometimes she still seemed to want to back him up, and more than once I'd heard her say that for all his flawed character my father had a good heart, and lived for us, would take the very bread out of his own mouth for us, and at Christmas spent all he had, and didn't have, on toys...

'But he's like my father-in-law,' my mother went on, talking to someone. 'He talks too much, gets wound up, loses control...'

I saw things differently. I thought that to him I was just a nuisance, that for some reason or other he didn't like me, and that he'd rather I'd never been born. If it had been me who'd died instead of the boy, this house would be a sea of calm, a little corner of peacefulness. They always said the boy was so fair, his eyes so blue he looked like an angel... Within me there was something which irritated him, something he deeply disliked. Maybe it was because I tended not to say very much and didn't feel like joking around. I don't know.

Finally, one Sunday afternoon we went to my Aunt's house after lunch to see the Traveller. My father shaved, twice over, washed from head to toe, changed his clothes and put brilliantine in his hair. My mother also put on her very best frock, and my shoes were polished and a hard collar put on my shirt. It had been some time since I'd felt this party mood, and although I wasn't thrilled at going to see the family, it was nice to see my father all clean, and more talkative.

My mother also looked wonderful. She'd done her hair, put a bit of powder on her face and had even used eyeliner. That day I had a really good feeling as I walked together with my parents, and I know I kept thinking that all the tension was just an unfortunate phase, and that like my mother said, my father had a good heart...

However the meeting was a disaster because, as we learned afterwards, Sebastià wasn't going to be there and it was all about Aunt Mercè's wanting, as she herself said, to get her brothers to make up. As a result there we were with Aunts Mercè and Carme, Uncle Pere, Auntie Neli, my two cousins, father, mother and me. My other cousin, Imma, wasn't there, and I don't recall Mercè's husband either, Uncle Ramon, who I heard had gone to get the car out of the garage, nor Auntie Lourdes.

Mercè had us sit in the conservatory, around a low table. As always, she was wearing a tight skirt which showed off an enormous arse, and a low-cut jumper. I saw she had freckles all over her skin. She was aloof with the maid, and tetchy...

'Girl,' she said to the young woman wearing a small white apron, 'did I just tell you to bring us the coffee here now?'

'Yes, Madam,' replied the girl. Mercè then added, 'Well don't just stand there gawping, we want it today...'

It had been some time since I'd seen Auntie Carme, and she looked better than before. She couldn't complain, she said, she had some good customers, the girl was working out well, but she couldn't forget about the night of the accident... Uncle Pere sat down on the other side of the table, some distance from us, and my mother took my cousin Esther's hand and asked her how she was.

'If we weren't all so pig-headed...' said Aunt Mercè at one point.

'Some more than others,' mumbled Uncle Pere, pretending to look out of the window; my father didn't respond.

I couldn't say for sure if the two of them really wanted to make up or not. Sometimes I got the impression they did, that they were tired of not having supper together and even not being able to argue with each other. But there were also other times when I thought the opposite, because my father behaved as if my uncle was dead, as if he'd never even existed. Once a neighbour asked my father after his brother.

'I haven't seen your brother for a while...' this lady said, and my father replied that his brother had been washed away by a riverful of shit. 'What a thing to say...' she said, and he just left her in mid-sentence. But then everyone knew him, and that he had these outbursts.

When the girl brought the coffee, my aunt poured it out. Each time she leant over, she displayed her breasts, which were also all freckled, until my father said, 'For God's sake, woman, you don't have to get your tits out just to pour the coffee...'

'There's no one around...' she said, to which he answered, 'Can't you see the boy's eyes are out on stalks?'

I could have died right there and then. I went red, my eyes welled up, and my head began to spin.

'Poor little thing,' she said to me, stroking my cheek. 'And Auntie's no spring chicken...'

Fortunately my mother asked me if I wanted a drop of milk, and the maid brought it over straight away. I don't know what they talked about after that. I had never hated my father like I did that afternoon. I thought of killing him, never speaking to him again, doing him every harm I could think of... I felt my cheeks on fire, and when I raised my eyes warily to look at him, the curious thing was that because he was so well dressed up I thought he looked kind, much kinder than at other times, even smiling and everything... But all I could do was repeat to myself that I could never forgive him for what he'd done to me, and that if he did anything like that ever again I'd leap on him, and hit him, even though he'd end up beating the shit out of me with those iron fists of his... The voices ringing out around me, voices ever more strident, made me lift my head up and suddenly I saw my father on his feet, shouting.

'That little shithead...' I thought he said to me, although actually he was talking about my uncle. 'He wants to turn me in...' he went on.

'You're an idiot...' responded my uncle calmly.

'Please don't fight, please,' said Auntie Carme. My cousin Lola started crying silently, next to her mother.

'Fuck you! Fuck the whole fucking lot of you!' screamed my father. And he indicated to my mother with a gesture that we were leaving.

Once we were out in the street, unlike on other occasions, my father seemed to have calmed down, and after a while he asked my mother, 'What do you make of them arseholes?' and my mother simply replied with a nod of her head in agreement.

Later on, as we got nearer home, my father said that to get all this shit about his brothers and sisters out of his hair we were going to have a bite to eat at the bar where he played cards. It was a big place, very near the Maragall Cinema. I'd never been inside, and to me it seemed full of smoke and noisy people. But as soon as my father started saying hello to people he seemed to forget about everything that had gone on at my aunt's house. He just looked to my mother now and then and asked her, 'Are you all right?' She replied that she was. 'It's because she's pregnant...' my father explained to everyone.

The waiter's name was Juanito, and my father was on very familiar terms with him. Juanito this, Juanito that. After a short while my father started laughing. I couldn't remember ever having seen him laugh like that, happy, content, liberated. My mother seemed like a duchess in that bar, in all her finery. Then the man who did the haulage for my father came up to the table. He smoked a lot, and had a glass of wine in his hand.

'My dear lady,' said the haulier, 'you have no idea how lucky you are to have such a husband. He can make a bit of money out of thin air...'

My father repeated what I'd heard him say before, 'When I've got some real cash I'm going to buy a house and put down a rug that's so thick that when my sisters come round they'll sink into it right up to their twats.'

He was like another person. He was friendly with the waiter, on first names with everyone, and even told a dirty joke that got the waiter laughing. The trucker, who was standing right by his side, put his arm affectionately round his shoulder and said he was a brilliant bloke.

Then up to the table came an old gent, who according to my father wrote novels about cops and robbers. He was a thin man, badly shaven and missing a lot of teeth, but I was just fascinated by the idea of being in the presence of someone who wrote books.

'What sort of thing do you like reading?' this man asked me. My mother answered that recently I couldn't keep away from books and even had one under my pillow. 'That's good,' said the thin man. 'When I was your age I'd never read a thing. But later on...'

The writer looked at me, taking his time over his brandy, sipping slowly. I wanted to ask him how you wrote a book, what you had to do to make up the story, if it was difficult to make the characters seem real... But I didn't dare say a word, because I couldn't understand how my father could know someone like this. It must have been then that I thought for the first time that maybe I could write too. I didn't tell anyone about it, didn't even talk to Joanet about it, but thought that as soon as I could find the time I'd start to tell the story, on a piece of paper, of a boy who lived in a country where it rained a lot, whose home was a big house surrounded by lavish gardens which he never left because he was ill. This lad would yearn to find out about the world outside the gardens, and because he wasn't able to, he would make it up. He made up what the houses were like, the streets, what the people were like... He made the whole thing up. The book would be called Running after Doves. I wouldn't even tell César about it, or Mrn Ronalia, not anyone. It would be my secret, the only serious thing in my life, which would allow me to put up with everything, having to work with my father, staying on at school a while longer, the brother that was going to be born...

In the dark, we went home under light rain. Halfway there my father gave me a little friendly slap on the back of my neck.

'How are you doing?' he asked me.

'Fine,' I replied. Nothing more.

My father had a few truly good days. It turned out suddenly that he knew people, was kind, and could even manage to display a certain tenderness... He did this through gestures that would have been imperceptible to anyone outside the family, but were nonetheless highly significant to us: when he walked alongside you he put his hand on your back; if you said anything he listened in silence; one evening he asked my mother if she fancied going to the pictures, and gave her more money than usual so she could pay off the debt at the shop...

'If only he was like this all the time, eh?' said my mother at one point.

And this is how it was: since the meeting at Aunt Mercè's house and going to the bar, my father finished work earlier, came to have supper with us and even, before bedtime, wanted me to go with him to the fountain to fill up a huge water container so my mother wouldn't have to go and fetch any all day. One evening, as we were filling the buckets we had to cart back, he turned to me and said:

'How are you doing?' And I replied again that everything was fine.

'Are you sure?' he insisted.

'Yes...' was my reply, more fearful than anything. And then after a while he asked me if I knew about the youngster who was going to be born, to which I replied that I did.

'Very good,' he said. 'You'll see how none of you will be wanting for anything...' he concluded.

He and I had never had such a long conversation, and on the way back to the house, with a bucket in each hand, I said to myself that it was fine by me this child coming along if it meant it brought all this with it... The next day I mentioned this to Joanet, who had some very clear ideas as far as adults were concerned, and he warned me, 'Don't count on it. Something'll happen to them and it'll all go back to being a pain in the arse, just like it was...'

But for a few days things worked out well, and it was hard to believe that this unknown peace had settled itself into our home. When I got back from school I was able to sit on my bed and put a rug over my knees, close my eyes and remember those first few lines of Defoe's book: *'It was about the beginning of September, 1664, that I, among the rest of my neighbours, heard in ordinary discourse that the plague was returned again in Holland...'*

I didn't dare open it and read on because I was afraid of breaking the spell. In fact I had enough with the opening, and didn't need to go further; as I continued to think about it I felt it increasingly just right, and it was easy for me to imagine the scene: as if he was talking about a time long past, when people dressed differently to us, like a film about pirates and wooden ships... And it was all set in a port city. I could see the misty, changeable damp September weather, a street full of people coming out of their houses and walking around... One group of people standing out from the rest. They were talking; in fact it was as if the camera zoomed in, as if it was showing me a close-up of the faces of these folk, one of whom was the man who was telling us this story... One of them had a big red nose, another had dark eyes, and there was a fat man with a faraway look... They spoke naturally about this plague business, that it was a dreadful thing, as if none of this horror could possibly affect them at all...

In the mornings, Joanet had started coming round to fetch me to go to school with him. It was as though I could sense when he was about to arrive, even before he got to the yard, and I'd say 'It's Joanet.' But my mother didn't realise I had this supernatural gift, and helped me on with my satchel as if nothing had happened. Then Joanet appeared, always more wrapped up than was necessary, and he'd say, 'Good morning.' I looked at my mother and she offered her cheek for me to kiss. She wasn't so thin, seemed prettier, and appeared happier.

'How's it going?' Joanet asked me as soon as we got outside. Knowing that he was talking about my father, I replied that everything was all right. 'You're so lucky...' And so we went to school slowly, hands in our pockets, not really feeling like talking at all. The truth is, though, that I really did feel fortunate, because if my father was okay, everything changed.

The only odd thing I detected those days was that my father deliberately changed the name for things. He didn't do it for a laugh, by which I mean it wasn't exactly a joke, but it wasn't because he got the name wrong either. This was his way of giving you a test, a kind of provocation which, if you couldn't handle it properly, could in other circumstances have had serious consequences. But as he was on a good run at the moment, as my mother put it, all it resulted in was a few anecdotes that Joanet couldn't quite understand.

'Pass me the baking powder...' my father would say, pointing at the salt cellar. My mother, who had developed a special sense for this sort of thing, knew what he meant. Or maybe he'd say, 'When you go out, put that blanket round your neck, my girl,' and my mother would have to tie a fine scarf over the neckline of her blouse because, according to my father, since she was pregnant everyone was looking at her breasts.

And then there were other things too, quite unimportant, but which I observed attentively, because any of these minutiae could give rise to this state of grace we were living in being wiped out. Of all of them, perhaps the most obvious were the glances, and the energy he put into things. The glances were certainly key. If he fixed his gaze on you, with his eyes open unnaturally wide, as if he were a bit mad, it meant it was all about to come to an end, even though he might still be joking around; if he set to work untiringly, doing more hours than anyone, going night after night without sleep, or went days without saying anything, then it was clear that the storm would erupt at any moment. He would suddenly look grim, suddenly seem exhausted and at the very limit of his strength, although this was only how it appeared, because actually his endurance was unimaginable. When he really couldn't keep going, he'd sleep for a while, then have a wash and suddenly seem rejuvenated. But he was unpredictable in everything. He could have a row with the lad who served the breakfast, and then with the man who went to grease the metal shutters... He always had reserves of energy to argue, to impose his own criteria, to furiously beat down his opponent... But at the same time he was completely overcome by weakness when someone in the family got ill. Then his look changed, he lost all colour from his lips, would tremble at anything, could cry like a child when someone he knew had a fever and the doctor said it might be pneumonia...

But instead of any of this happening, my father started making rather strange decisions. The most surprising was that Auntie Lourdes went to work for him; that's to say she went and spent her day at the sorting table selecting bits of cloth. She'd had some sort of problem with Auntie Carme, and my father took advantage of this to offer her the work. As he was getting more customers all the time, he had to go out and see people to buy or to sell, such that he needed someone to go through the stocks, and keep an eye on the warehouse. What's more, as I heard him say at home one night, it would also succeed in pissing off his sisters, and his little brother.

Sometimes, when they finished at the warehouse, my father brought my aunt to our house for supper. Then my mother would have to get ready a bowl of warm water so she could wash, and she'd spend an hour at the table putting on powder, then dark eye shadow and finally brilliant red lipstick. She did this slowly, without a word, in silence, because she was tired and didn't have the energy to open her mouth, as she explained the first day.

Perhaps she was nicer than the other aunties, but at the time she didn't seem so in the slightest. My mother wasn't impressed either at having another person to cook for, but since we were enjoying this better period she didn't say anything. When my father wasn't around she just let slip, very nonchalantly, a few stories about Aunt Lourdes so I could hear. That she wasn't seeing the married man who'd kept her any more, that she'd had a row with Aunt Carme and didn't want to help out at the hairdresser's any more, that she didn't have any skills, had never worked and had been to see Uncle Sebastià for advice... So the idea that she should work with my father came from Sebastià, and wasn't a bad one because that way my father had someone he could trust helping him, and it only took a moment to learn the job...

'What I bet Sebastià didn't say,' my mother said, 'was for her to come here to wash, because I'm the one who has to go and get the water in... And he won't have said she should be round here all the time for supper, either...'

This auntie amused me because she was pretty ugly, but still took great care over her appearance. As well as all the time she spent in front of the mirror, there was what she did with her clothes: once she'd put her face on she changed her clothes and dressed herself up as if she was going to a wedding, and actually all she was going to do was have supper with us. My mother always said to her, 'How smart you look...' to which she would reply, 'Oh no my dear, just a couple of old things...'

In fact these days, except for all this with Auntie Lourdes, it seemed to me as if life had stopped. I didn't read, and did absolutely nothing at school; when Joanet and I went out to the playground we just sat and chatted, at lunchtime I ate without saying anything to my mother, and the afternoons in the classroom were crushingly endless, the tedious nonsense and cracked voice of the teacher...

In the evenings, when school was out, we went home as slowly as we possibly could. We stopped off at Ramon's parents' pulse shop. Ramon wore a beige coverall and with his bright smile served the customers with considerable skill. But obviously he didn't have time for us, and we'd arrange to meet at the table-football bar on the Saturday evening although more often than not he didn't turn up. Antonio on the other hand sometimes came to the school to meet us. The three of us then started walking and he said he'd been sent out on an errand and was spinning it out before he went back to work... He said again he was sick of being ordered around, that the ironmonger's was a den of arseholes and that there was a small thin man there who was a National and kept an eye on all the others. What he said was that they had a thing about him and more than once had threatened to fire him. He also knew some people in the market who had a fish stall. They'd offered him a job there selling, but he'd have to get up at five in the morning, and didn't know what he should do...

'The bugger about working,' he said again, 'is you can never get away from it. It's with you all the time... That's why I can see Salvador's got it better than us, still at school, even though his father doesn't even let him have a sniff of the street with all this draughtsman shit...'

Antonio and Joanet concurred that life was shit and they'd rather never have been born. I didn't know what to think. When my father was not all right, when he'd gone off his rails as my mother put it, and went savage, nothing at all was easy, but there were still things I liked to find out about, for example the conversations you could have with César or Mrs Rosalia, or even going to the bar with my father and seeing close up what someone who wrote books was like. I don't know, I just liked musing over such things, thinking that maybe this writer Defoe was also an old toothless man who

130

went to bars... But there was always the chance things could suddenly get turned on their head, and become unbearable.

I felt I wanted to see César, but since I hadn't progressed any further in my reading of the book, I was embarrassed to go and see him and say I'd only read three lines and that had been enough, that I felt vividly involved in it although I'd ventured no further than those first words that I knew by heart... 'It was about the beginning of September, 1664, that I, among the rest of my neighbours, heard in ordinary discourse that the plague was returned again in Holland...' Besides I couldn't tell them, or anybody else, that I spent my time watching my father and Aunt Lourdes, checking on what I called the domestic pulses, the rhythmic variations that allowed me to know in advance when a storm was about to erupt... Neither could I explain to them that it wasn't important in itself that my father changed the name for things, but rather the kind of false name he chose... If he wanted to tell my mother to switch off the radio and said, 'Turn that saucepan off...' there wasn't much danger. If on the other hand he said, 'Turn that machine off...' we could start trembling. Maybe it was because machines got on his nerves, as much as it did if he had to go down to the depot to get ice because he hadn't been ready when the truck came round... Whatever, the saucepan was inoffensive, and the machine wasn't.

All told, those days went by without any great hitches, and more than anything I lived on the lookout for these sorts of indicators. I even came up with a theory, based in part on what Joanet said, that when nothing special was going on you'd better get yourself ready for the big one.

'It's always like that,' said Joanet. 'When everything's going well, that's when I start to shudder...'

And at home the only tension you could sense was not being able to see Uncle Pere, Aunt Neli and my cousins. My aunt in fact did come sometimes behind my father's back, when he was at work, but Uncle Pere never dared. Apparently things weren't going well for him, and my father's merriness was partly down to his brother's getting it wrong with a couple of purchases and losing quite a lot of money.

'Old sonny boy Pere...' said my father, with a mocking sing-song in his voice, 'he's really put his foot in it again. They've palmed off such a heap of shit on him he won't be able to scrape it off his shoes for years... But then of course he's such a genius...'

Despite everything they started to miss each other, and months before Christmas my father was already saying that we'd see what happened next year, because the way things were going, if the moron didn't give an inch... It was the first serious alarm call. If he got obsessed about something, started going on and on about the same claptrap, only referring to my uncle as the moron – the moron says this, the moron's done that, I've no idea what the moron's on about – that meant we were going to have a problem very soon.

One Saturday afternoon Joanet and I went to see César. We knew that on that day of the week he was always there after lunch, because he liked to have a little lie down, a little snooze, and then settle down to read. We did indeed find him sitting on the bench outside in the sun, with a book in his hands, and he seemed happy to see us. He started talking glowingly about his mother, who had gone with Mr Gaspar to see a friend of theirs who was ill. What he told us was that as well as French, Catalan and Spanish, his mother spoke Italian and a bit of Russian. She'd taken up Russian because she wanted to read Tolstoy in the original, but then she'd got this eye problem, and thought that if she was going to lose her sight, as the doctors had warned her, she'd rather spend her time reading than learning languages. She was a lady who could talk about anything, said César, and that while most people went for Poe for his horror stories, she liked him for his book *Eureka*. She knew the names of lots of plants in Latin, which César said was the language the priests spoke; she knew the habits of birds, knew stories of the Greek Gods, and could recite, in German, some of Zarathustra's speeches, especially the one she liked the most: 'Of all that is written, I love only what a person hath written with his blood. Write with blood, and thou wilt find that blood is spirit.'

'That's important,' César told us, 'although it certainly is hard to understand. Look: reading is absolutely essential for humans, but there comes a point where you can't just read any old thing. That's when you choose, and if you go for culture, the accumulation of knowledge, then you're lost. You have to learn to give up all those things and take the path of blood, the path of difficult truth, the hardest, the path that understands the spirit as a profoundly sincere exaltation...'

'You mean you don't have to learn anything at school then?' I asked him spontaneously.

'Well, in a certain way, yes. And I'm sure that if people heard me telling you that, they'd accuse me of leading you down the wrong path. But you understand me, don't you?'

'I think so...' I replied.

Joanet was looking at us, surprised, and at one point stated that he didn't understand many of the things we were saying, and in fact didn't want to try. He'd realised quite well enough that very soon he'd come across people who wouldn't do him any good and take him up dead ends... He'd let himself be led, because that's what life was like, letting yourself be led to places that didn't do you any good.

'Look at Antonio, and Perico too... What's happened to them? I mean, that's what I'm talking about. And the same thing's going to happen to us...'

'Come on, not necessarily...' said César.

But Joanet was decided. He'd been in a bad way for some time, and had no illusions. His mother always said the lad seemed like an old man, talked like an old man, and in truth he himself often said he was tired and lived in a state of fatigue that sleep couldn't get rid of.

'The only thing I like is being with you,' he said to César and me that day.

César asked us if we'd go with him to sell paper, and the three of us went out to the yard with piles of old newspapers that he gathered up from all over the place. We tied them tightly with white string and when we had five or six packets we stacked them into what was left of an old pram onto which César had added a wooden crate. The wheels were knackered but turned well enough. And so, pushing this contraption, which amused Joanet and me, we set off down the street to the rag and bone man's place.

It was a small shop, full of paper and bits of iron, old photographs, worn-out clothes... The rag and bone man had a set of scales a bit like my father's, possibly even smaller, and on them he weighed the paper César had brought him. They did a few sums, and then César said he'd take us for something to eat with the money he'd made. We went into a bar where Joanet and I shared a cheese sandwich and César ate a plateful of tripe and chickpeas. We drank water, but he had a glass of wine. As we ate, the conversation returned to all the things César's mother knew about, and the importance of the choice of one book or another.

'My mother always says the same thing,' said César, whose attitude made him seem one of us, despite the difference in age, though he had more things in his head and more experience. 'She always says that the importance of literature doesn't originate from the theme, but rather the way it's told. And I think she's right. What do you think?' he asked us, and Joanet and I just sat there stunned, because no one had ever asked us anything quite like that question before.

'No idea,' said Joanet, with a smile I hadn't seen in a long time. 'I'm not even sure if I know what you're talking about...'

'It's just a question of thinking. When someone tells you about a fact, something that's happened, don't you find it's important how he tells you about it?'

'Obviously...' I answered.

'Well that's the answer to what I was saying. A book is never just the story it tells. It's how it's told. There's an author called Azorín who can write pages and pages about what an apple's like...'

This last bit really amused us and Joanet and I looked at each other. An apple, Joanet said, is an apple, and it's not exactly difficult to describe. César disputed this. According to him, an apple, just the skin of an apple, can have a series of qualities that a good writer has to be able to make stand out. The shine of the skin, the shade of green, yellow or red, its ripeness or lack of it... But aside from all this about the apple, it was true that I myself had found something special in those first lines of that book about the plague that I couldn't read, as if the words said more than they actually did if you read them one by one... And then without a thought I remember I came out, quite spontaneously, with this comment: 'You know that book you lent me? Well now I can't read it, but it's like I have been reading without opening it at all... I want to read it so much that when I do I'll already know it...'

And César, unlike what would have happened at home or at school, or even with the lads in the gang, thought that what I was saying was perfectly reasonable and understandable.

'That happens sometimes,' he said, 'but still, you mustn't think it'll always be like that. And you should know very clearly what's stopping you from reading.'

'It's because my mother's going to have a baby, and nowadays I go to the fountain with my father to get the water, and I help out more than I used to...'

I was a little embarrassed at having said that, though Joanet already knew about it and he and I had talked more than once about what was going on with me because of the baby; how I could barely think about it because those sad days of intense heat when my other brother died just filled my head... César also said something perfectly understandable. 'I've never really got on with my sister. All this about you've got to love your brothers and sisters is sometimes true and sometimes not at all. It all depends on lots of factors.'

It was precisely that which drew us to him: he said things in a different way; in his words it all seemed different, as though he spoke the truth, didn't deceive us at all...

That same afternoon, when Joanet and I left César at his home, we started talking about these things in a way that we hadn't done for some time. First of all we thought it was fantastic that he'd invited us for a sandwich, and we also agreed as we so often had that it was impossible to talk with our parents like we did with César, who while he wasn't old enough to be our father wasn't far off it. But then, suddenly, as we were walking along, I noticed that Joanet had become sad again, his spirits couldn't cope, his eyes had become glassy, as if he was going to start crying.

'You know what, I don't want to live...' he said, to which I replied that I didn't either. Joanet, however, was telling the truth and I wasn't. Two days later he threw himself onto the railway tracks in front of one of those long noisy goods trains we used to enjoy watching go by.

All this with Joanet was terrible for everyone. The neighbourhood was in a real commotion over what that lad had done, but nobody asked me or César anything at all. If they had we would have explained that Joanet just couldn't go on, that he was crushed by a great sadness, a sadness which made him live in fear and had pushed him little by little towards the tracks... In fact, we ourselves hadn't realised this. We hadn't noticed that through the conversations César and I had, we were continually leaving him more and more alone. Joanet and I went out walking, we told each other things, but within me I had essentially shifted towards César. I had the hope of books, the dream of reading, the drive to learn new things. He on the other hand had ended up on his own, could barely share things with us and had taken refuge in a discreet and silent sadness.

The day of the burial, Joanet's mother was dressed all in black, and looked about to faint, with no colour in her face, and she just wept, saying over and over something like, 'Why did you do it, why did you do it...?' In contrast, his father and brother seemed not to have realised Joanet was dead. His father didn't know where to put himself or what to do, and his brother even smiled when people extended their hand to express their condolences, as if for once in his life he felt important.

I was with the boys of the group. Perico and Antonio looked shocked. Ramon brushed his hair from his forehead and couldn't keep still. Salvador came in a jacket and tie. Miquel's eyes were bigger and darker than ever. Daniel was thin, pale. Jaume put on the Falangist uniform and stood there strong the whole time... I felt César behind me, and his putting a hand on my shoulder. *He* knew the truth. I lifted my eyes to look at him. I remember we were on the point of crying and that he stroked my hair. I felt a great suffering for Joanet, and awash with this emotion, said to myself that I would become César's son. With the gentle gesture of touching my hair, he took me in, and I understood perfectly what he was trying to tell me. I was completely indifferent to my aunts, uncles, cousins, the brother on the way, my father... The lads of the group meant little, either. The only ones who counted were my dead brother, Joanet, César and to an extent my mother, because somehow she seemed as sad as poor Joanet. The rest had no value of any sort.

Then the priest delivered a long homily saying this had been a tragic accident for the family and friends of this kind-hearted boy. A simple family who couldn't understand why God had subjected them to such a severe test. But who were we to understand God, whose designs inevitably were beyond us...

As I heard these slow sentences ring out in the church, I told myself that this had been no accident. Some men had seen it all: Joanet waiting, up against the wall on the platform, and as he heard the train approaching, moving forward slowly toward the track. At one moment they called out because they'd worked out what was about to happen and then Joanet disappeared, just as though some guardian angel had gathered him up and taken him straight off to heaven. Everybody had abandoned him, even César and I, I, his friend...

Afterwards we all went to the Poblenou cemetery. Walking down the pathways, graves on either side, the silence and the mixed scents of flowers and humidity made you queasy. In front of me Perico walked with difficulty, his leg rigid. Ramon kept his hands in his pockets and looked respectfully at the photographs on the graves. I didn't see the other lads of the group, but I knew they were among the people there. In his own way, Joanet had surprised us because we'd never have thought he'd leave us unable to breathe. Later, when they'd placed the coffin in the grave, my father said, 'That's that,' and wanted to go and see the boy.

At my brother's grave, where there were no photographs or flowers, my mother started to cry, her head resting on my father's arm. Her belly was very noticeable, despite the big coat she was wearing. My feet were cold, and I felt not a tear, no feeling whatsoever, dry, absurdly hard. My mother's weeping seemed false, lying, as lying as the words of the priest, or the condolences of the teacher, who had always hated Joanet but instead made up who knows what... But these were lies that somehow were harmful, because everyone was serious, everyone seemed polite, and what's more, the cemetery exerted its own powerful effect. So I felt tense, and couldn't understand why, when we'd gone to bury a friend, we'd ended up crying at the child's grave, or why I was having these thoughts with not a hint of emotion...

But that night, and the following ones, I dreamt strange things. I saw Joanet near the tracks, smiling and waving goodbye until the long noisy goods train which took him away went past. I then saw a white coffin on one of the tables in the bar, and when I approached it I discovered Joanet and my brother inside, one beside the other, in each other's arms, as if they were asleep. A moment later Joanet was sitting at the foot of my bed, covered in bloodstains, telling me in a distant moan of a voice not to be afraid, that he wasn't dead, he'd only done it because he was sick of everything and everyone, but we were friends, and every so often he'd come round to fetch me so we could go and see César.

'But none of that making excuses so you can sit on your own reading, okay? You see, I know everything now...' And he told me off with a wag of a long, broken finger.

In the mornings, when I woke up, I felt tired and had the sensation I'd been left totally alone in the world. I felt no pain, but had no desire to get up. I recalled the walks he and I took those cold afternoons on the way home from school, what he'd told me of his brother, the bitterness and sadness he'd lived in those last months, with nobody realising... Now it was I who didn't know what to do, or who to turn to. There were times I imagined him happy, relieved of the heavy weight that had become unbearable to him. It was logical that he'd moved forward slowly towards the tracks; maybe he'd been planning it for a long time, and who knows whether he'd somehow put off the end so he could keep me company...

But the worst was at school. Although we sat a long way away from each other in class, we got together at break time and spent the time watching the little kids and younger boys, who still had to spend years in that prison. They all wore those striped smocks done up at the collar, and very short hair. The two of us had long trousers, but there were some in golfing knickerbockers or short trousers. Often he and I didn't say a word during these recreation periods, and when we had to go back to the classroom, we took leave of each other with just a little nod of the head, but at going home time we always made our way back to our houses together. So for days and days I couldn't take my eyes off the seat that had been left empty in the classroom. And when I went down to the playground I sat on the steps, heard the hubbub of kids playing, saw the wild chestnut trees, the fountain... I told myself Joanet was just ill, and would be back in a few days. Later I realised that no, I would never see him nor my brother ever again, this was for always, and I didn't know what to do.

What's more, because my father was earning a little more money than before, he signed me up for extra revision classes and one evening as I was going home I found the streets even colder, darker and lonelier than ever. At that moment I would have given anything to have Joanet by my side, be able to talk to him, and see him smile even if it was just for a moment.

The cold slowly settled in at home, in the streets and at school. It was a damp cold that seized your flesh, and there was no way of avoiding it. In the evenings, before I went to bed, my mother put two hot water bottles between the sheets, and in the middle of winter I was even allowed to go to bed with my socks on, but the bottles went cold straight away and I had to get them out with my feet, and however many blankets I put on I just couldn't get warm. Sometimes I managed to make myself a nest in the bed, a tepid nook exactly following the shape of my body, and I lay there, immobile, barely daring to breathe. I'd always thought that if I kept still, bad things wouldn't happen. You had to keep a low profile so my father wouldn't lose his rag, you had to keep clear of certain places so the Falangists didn't fix their eyes on you, at school you had to keep quiet to save yourself problems, it was best not to play in the playground to make sure you didn't hurt yourself, or get a tear in your clothes...

All the same, however low a profile you kept, you couldn't avoid this hard season of cold, wind, rain and damp arriving every year. Or that equally horrible one of heat that turned the house into a dreadful oven, and made us live more outside than in. Whatever, the worst for me was winter. The damp, and the leaks, it all made me feel defenceless, and though I didn't realise at the time, it humiliated me. In our street everyone lived in single-storey houses, except Salvador who had a little house on two floors, but we didn't have running water, and however much effort my mother put into keeping it in order...

Every year, when the bad weather arrived, the subject of the house always came up one way or another. Sometimes it was Aunt Neli who brought it up, being more impulsive than my mother, saying we had to have a good think about this, that if we went on living like this we'd make ourselves ill. My father then gave her a good stare, and with a laughably mad face on him said yes, his bollocks would definitely make themselves ill... To which she replied, 'Look sonny, go shove it up your pretty little arse.'

But that year, because my father and Uncle Pere hadn't made up, it was my mother who mentioned it. It had definitely started to get cold, and everyone was saying we were in for a long difficult winter.

'We might even get snow...' she'd heard a neighbour say.

Bearing in mind that in a few months' time the baby

would arrive, you could understand my mother starting with the same old stuff, talking about it in a roundabout way and doing strange things. For example, at bedtime she put more blankets than ever on my bed and virtually every day at suppertime asked me if I was cold, and brought the oil heater closer. My father gave her a sideways look and said nothing. A little while later, she brought the subject up again: a neighbour had told her the rain was going to be really heavy this year, and someone else had been going on about snow too...

'If it's cold,' said my father, half angrily, 'we'll burn the furniture and get warm.' My mother replied, 'Oh come on... you can't say a thing, can you? All I was saying was...'

In fact, though, this was the best moment to be talking about it, because my father was in a pretty good mood, always saying things were going well, and that soon we'd be back on our feet and then they'd start ringing the bells. He was in such a good mood that one Sunday evening at suppertime he appeared in the dining room in his underwear, with his arms stretched out in front of him, dead parallel, lumbering along like Frankenstein's monster.

'You'll catch cold,' said my mother with a laugh, and then, still clowning around, he turned slowly toward the bedroom, wailing like a ghost. 'If only he was always like this...' murmured my mother. The fact was that ever since the break with my uncle, he really did seem calmer and less aggressive, sometimes surprising us with jokes like this.

Anyway, at the beginning of that winter the subject of the house came up again. I, for whatever reason, actually felt the cold as I never had before. I saw it in the walls, and when I put my hand there, I felt it first in my palm, and then this dampness crept up my arm till it got to my back, from where it plunged shuddering through my entire body. Perhaps people were right when they said we ought to prepare for a dreadful winter... Maybe I just noticed the chill in the house and felt it more. Whatever, my father started talking about a house he'd been told about near where we lived, a big house, two floors, very good condition, running water, yard out the back.... My mother always said 'It doesn't need to be that grand... just so long as it's got running water and doesn't leak...'

And without realising it, we found ourselves talking more and more about moving house. Sometimes my mother and father argued a bit, my father would get angry and walk out slamming the door, but it was nothing like what we'd gone through previously, when things were going wrong and screams and fights broke out over nothing.

But along with all this, I couldn't get out of the sadness that Joanet's death had caused in me. In fact I felt more lonely than ever, and all sorts of worries started prowling around in me. First I thought I'd tell my mother I wanted to go out to work. Doing something new would be good for me, but there was always the danger that my father would say I had to go and work for him, and that would get me nowhere. I also thought of talking to Jaume and hanging around the Falangist place, secretly of course, but I was scared because my father always said that if those bastards ever turned their sights back on us we'd be really stuffed... I could also ask if I could continue my studies and get more friendly with Salvador, but I didn't want to do that, and anyway my father said that too much studying made you go queer and he'd learned everything at the university of life, so it was virtually certain he'd say no. Occasionally all that stuff about being sent off to the island would come back into my mind... This idea danced around in my head for days and days. Depending on the moment I might think it was just right, the best thing that could possibly happen, and at others it made no sense whatsoever: I didn't know anyone there and I'd be even lonelier than ever...

I missed Joanet of course in other ways, such as our visits together to César's house. I'd stopped going there, since he'd gone. I sometimes thought about the old people, but it was exactly the same as thinking about my friends around town. They were there, they lived near us, I knew them, could talk to them, but for a number of reasons they were no longer within reach. They had died with Joanet, they'd vanished, they'd gone with him to heaven or wherever... When I came out of school I walked deliberately where it was muddiest, and when I got home my mother yelled at me not to come in with those shoes on and told me off for getting them soaked. I took them off, cleaned them with a stick and then left them to dry. The next morning I wiped them with a dry cloth and coated them with a bit of polish but by the evening they were the same as before, because it rained a lot and the streets were a mess.

One evening, coming out of school, I started crying in a doorway. It was all very sudden, just like that, but I wasn't surprised because I realised I'd been carrying these tears inside me for years. I cried for everything and for everyone, and as I cried I felt that with this sobbing and trembling an important part of my childhood was disappearing.

'I'm growing up,' I told myself, 'I've got to learn how to be a grown-up... I want to be strong like Daniel...' But I didn't know how. Afterwards, wiping my eyes with a handkerchief, I thought my face must be dirty. I washed in the fountain and at home they had no idea because my father was doing his accounts with my mother sitting beside him in case she had to help.

'If I could read...' I told myself when I got into my room. But all I could do was wait, lie there on my bed and wait, for whatever.

Occasionally I went by Pere's Bar and sometimes ran into Pulico there, standing in the doorway, looking out on to the street. Since his operation he hadn't been to work two days in a row, and whenever he could he complained about the pain his leg gave him, the doctors, and every bloody thing under the sun. According to him, Joanet had done the right thing when he'd shuffled off this mortal coil. The life we'd been dealt was shit, and it was a shame the war hadn't done away with everything... Then he had a glass of white wine and added, 'I'm always going to be a cripple, you know what I mean? Well fuck it! Let the whores do their work.' He stood there at the door, doing absolutely nothing.

I remembered him just a few years before, when despite the pain with his leg he used to run around and jump about like crazy, and loved doing things to wind people up. Once he, Jaume and Ramon trussed up Daniel, who started crying like a little girl when he saw his hands and feet all tied together... Another time he shat in the entrance to the building where the lady who taught French lived, and he was a very good shot when it came to breaking windows... But lately he'd not wanted to lift a finger, looked bitter, and sometimes went to the Falangist place on the pretext of seeing Jaume.

In fact that winter the whole neighbourhood ground to a halt. It rained, it was hard to get heating oil, the streets were empty, wet, there were more power cuts than ever... As it was dark when I came out of school, I couldn't go and visit César, and on Saturdays I had to go and fetch the water, then my father wanted me to go with him to the warehouse... Actually, I couldn't find the right moment to go and see the old people. I thought that without Joanet, even they would send me packing, because I still hadn't started reading the book about the plague, and never had anything to say... As the days passed, it became more and more difficult for me to bring myself to go and see them. But luckily, one evening when I was coming home from school, I saw César at the door to our house, as though he was waiting for me. He had the sole of his shoe, and his back, against the wall, and when I saw him my heart leapt with happiness. He was also pleased and started telling me he'd changed jobs and was working in a textile factory now, that it was a good firm, and that we hadn't been able to see each other until then because of all these changes.

'How are you?' he asked then, to which I replied that I was fine. 'Sure?' he asked, and I answered yes.

It was curious that César, who was much older than me – he must have been about thirty – and who'd read so many books and knew so many things, was interested in talking to me. But he'd come looking for me, was kind, and that same afternoon talked to me for a while about this new job he had. The owner of the factory was a man called Mr. Pàmies, short, slim, always with colour in his face because he liked playing tennis. The first morning Mr Pàmies had shaken him by the hand, and told him that in this company everyone enjoyed their work. Then there was Josep, the foreman, who had a Jewish nose, and Esteve who was tall and blonde, and did the accounts in an office, assisted by a long-haired girl called Marta. There was also Quim who although still young had grey hair, and had a lot of contact with the blue-coated women who did the weaving because he did the maintenance on the machines, as well as weaving. One of these girls was called Dolores; she was the oldest and had been in the firm longest. Then there was Pilar who was blonde and always wore her hair back, and Maria who was little, dark skinned and talked all the time, Roser who was tall and serious with curly hair, and finally Mercè, who was quite fat and very pale skinned... According to César it was always hot inside the factory, and the women would sometimes raise their arms in such a way that you could see a bit of their thighs. The worst thing was the never-ending deafening noise, the sort of constant rhythmic hammering that meant you had to speak loudly, almost shouting just to say anything. But most of his work was in the storerooms, where it was a little quieter. With the doors closed the noise was a kind of distant hum, unceasing but muffled. At times he could even read. He sat half hidden among the boxes and shelves and read for two or three hours at a time. If anyone came in he immediately heard the door and hid the book, and in fact so far they hadn't caught him... He looked happy about this job, and told me from his mother that on Saturday afternoon I could go round to their house, because they wanted to see me...

This conversation helped me to get over the sadness of not having Joanet, helped me not to think so much about his death, about my being responsible, and the dreadful moment when he went towards the tracks, and like a gust of wind the train carried him away for ever. I felt I could breathe more easily, fill my lungs with a cleaner purer air, because at home, despite my mother's neatness, I always had the sensation of living in a foul atmosphere of various bad smells: my father's tobacco, the farts he let off, the dust he brought in from the warehouse, the damp of the walls... My father also got into the habit of bringing old things home. One day he arrived with some straw-coloured napkins with flowers embroidered on them that must have come from some dark and distant past. My mother thought they were as revolting as I did, but he said they were old, really expensive, and we should wash and keep them. Another day he turned up with a suitcaseful of Zorro novels and cops and robbers stories. And he brought in a broken figurine of a ballet dancer, even more crippled than Perico... This sickened me, and above all made me nervous because my father forgot about it straight away, which allowed my mother to hide it in some corner or other of the house, not daring to throw it out in case he ever remembered it. This feeling was the same as the one I'd had for years when I went to the barber's round the corner, where the floor was covered in hair, the sheets they swaddled you up in weren't quite white, always stained and creased, where the mouldering mirrors were full of little black holes that seemed like bad omens...

That night, instead of dreaming about poor Joanet, I returned to seeing Edir the giant, trying to stand up straight, Mrs Rosalia carefully sniffing the flowers, and Mr Gaspar sitting in the yard, smoking. I saw them as though it was summertime, as though the weather was good, as though we were all calm, without worries, enjoying the tranquillity and warmth of the sun, letting the time go by peacefully. And nothing had happened; the boy hadn't died, nor had Joanet, my gang of friends didn't go out to work, Perico hadn't grown that dreadful moustache and didn't spend all his time at Pere's Bar doing nothing, Uncle Esteve hadn't been killed in the car, Auntie Lourdes didn't come to our house so often, we saw Uncle Pere and Aunt Neli, it wasn't cold, the blasts of icy wind didn't blow in through the joints in the windows, penetrating my soul...

But when I put my feet back on the floor it was like ice, and the warm milk my mother gave me was horrible, she looked tired, my father had already left, the way to school was endless, unpleasant, ugly, and the day dragged on and on. What I liked most, really, was listening. I'd always listened as much as I could. When we went outside in summer to get fresh air I listened to the older people. They'd suddenly start laughing at nothing, and I watched them in silence. And I wasn't the only one in the family who said very little. People said that Uncle Pere and my father were very similar, but I thought they were quite different. My uncle was quieter, and sometimes went for hours without saying anything.

'Today he's playing dumb,' I'd heard Aunt Neli say when they'd been for supper and he didn't even say as much as a hello.

'Just as well for you,' my mother'd replied.

There was also the case of Uncle Sebastià, a man of few words, and Aunt Mercè's husband, who couldn't even open his mouth because she immediately butted in. Or the case of Salvador's father, who because of the work he did listened and kept his mouth shut, as Salvador himself told me. But when I kept quiet, I did so to learn something, did so because the absence of sound opened up my surroundings, turning them into clear space. The din of the school when we all went down the stairs, for example, was sordid and chaotic. On the other hand if you had to go somewhere on your own, if you left the classroom and went down the stairs alone, every little detail took on its own importance: the light coming in from outside, casting shadows on the steps and walls, the sound you made with your hand on the bannister, the indistinct silhouette of someone moving stealthily around the ground floor, the inaudible squeak of your shoe... I'd sometimes stopped to take in these miracles of silence and calm. The fine dust floating in the rays of sunlight, the cold shadows hiding in the stairwell, the wide endless corridor disappearing into the light, a door closing far away, resonating from the upper floor... I went down slowly, gently pushed by a friendly hand, and in my movements I possessed the entire school, the street even; and then the brick fortress, wrapped up in clouds and mud, sad-faced, eyes shut, could raise itself up into the air, and smile at me as I moved around its silent entrails.

Other people, like Ramon, preferred hustle and bustle. He was waiting excitedly for the Clot Fiestas. He took everyone along with him to the whirl of spinning carousels, flying swings, the uproar of the grown-ups with their air rifles, the strident music that got Perico all excited and froze an envious smile onto Antonio's face. We didn't have the money to go on any of the rides, obviously, but the fairground stalls enthralled us, and we would have given absolutely anything to be able to go into the big top tent. The grown-ups themselves got carried away by the fair, laughing and going around till their legs went weak. I quickly felt this dizziness, and the dust of so many feet made my nose itch.

So that Saturday I rushed off to César's house, and when the old lady saw me she came up and put a hand of pure bone on my back, and kissed me on the cheek.

'How come you've been so long?' she asked me.

She was happy to see me, as was Mr Gaspar, who in his own way, without moving from the corner of the table where he was sitting, appeared to smile. We talked then about

Joanet, and Mrs Rosalia said something unusual. 'Only those favoured by the Gods die young...'

She was always coming out with things like this. Most people said poor lad, so young, must have been an accident... She spoke of Gods, or said of Joanet's mother, 'She's the one who's suffering the most. She's left with no future.'

It was a wonderful afternoon, and later on, as I was leaving to go home, even Edir the giant, sitting in the same armchair as ever, tried to give me a swipe on the backside with his newspaper, as if he too was glad I'd come back.

Under the Dust

From then on, every Saturday afternoon I went to see Mrs Rosalia, Mr Gaspar, César and Edir. Sitting down with them around the table transported me into a new world. I smelled perfectly the stink of the oil and the scorched wick of the lamp. Along with that, because of the dirt and damp in the house, the sole of my shoe sometimes got a bit stuck to the floor. When they opened the window that gave on to the passageway, I noticed there were cobwebs on the ceiling and that the walls hadn't been painted for years and years... Ramon had said all this the first time they'd gone to the old people's house, and had also said he didn't want to go back there because there were bugs and fleas in that hole. But I didn't care about all of this, because I found everything about the old people interesting, and whatever it was that we were talking about I soon felt no embarrassment in asking about anything I didn't understand. Without realising it, I started to live the stories they told me, as if they were my own life: I was Robinson, I was the usurer's assassin, I stowed away on a ship, hidden in the hold... During the week, César had to get up early because the textile factory where he worked opened up at seven, and it was up in Gràcia. He had to get the metro, and then he still had a way to walk. His job consisted of looking after the stores, making up the labels, carrying the crates of yarn to the machines, and he had to collect up the empty bobbins, bits of paper and other rubbish that accumulated. On the first few days the supervisor, Josep, wanted him to watch closely how it all worked. César had to familiarise himself with the machines and the girls who operated them.

Something else they talked about was the story of Edir, the giant who existed in the armchair, next to a pile of yellowed newspapers, his feet swollen and his clothes stained. Edir, said Mr Gaspar, had been a businessman. Before the war he was always coming back and forth from London, and although Mr Gaspar didn't know any of the details, he was apparently involved in the export and import of various kinds of merchandise. At that time, Edir lived in an apartment in the Eixample area, was married, and had two children. He was a tall man, always well-dressed and elegant... On more than one occasion he'd asked Mr Gaspar, whom he'd known since they were young, to go up to Perpignan just to deliver a suitcase to a hotel porter. Mr Gaspar, who was a journalist back then, had to make ends meet by doing little jobs from time to time that he didn't ask too many questions about.

'Best thing is to do what you're told and keep your mouth shut...' he'd often say.

'But that way you never know what you're getting

154

yourself into, do you?' Mrs Rosalia would point out, to which César would respond with a smile and Mr Gaspar with a dismissive gesture, or by lighting a cigarette with two or three puffs, which, due to his not having any teeth left, meant stretching his lips.

They said that Edir's good times originated from the First World War, and I liked hearing about a war of which I knew nothing at all, and which I deduced from his words had been even worse than our war and the World War that had ended not long before

'The horror of the twentieth century probably begins with the Great War,' Mrs Rosalia went on, 'and from out of its great ills the delirium of fascism emerged, with the consequences of which we are still living.'

Edir suffered a financial reverse and lost everything: his business, wife, children... It all collapsed like a house of cards. He became ill and after spending months in hospital – a period when he was visited regularly only by Mr Gaspar, who was grateful to him for the times that he'd given him a bit of work, and the blonde woman who still went to see him sometimes – he found himself on the street, alone, with absolutely nothing and nowhere to go for shelter. At that point Mr Gaspar took him in to his house, the only way he could, offering him the corner of the entranceway, and that's where he ended up, thinking it would just be a matter of a few days. But then the war came, they went hungry, and when the Nationals won, Edir was still with them, sitting in that chair, a little worse every day.

'He lives sitting down, obviously, but he can't lie down either,' said Mrs Rosalia. 'He'd suffocate.'

I felt clearly that these dirty, poor people were my family, my friends, my life, and I wouldn't have changed them for anything in the whole world. They transported me into the land of words, of new stories, a life of variety forever to be discovered, with a past, present and future, with hope, with good and with bad, with memories, smells and feelings.

'What I remember about Algeria,' said Mrs Rosalia from time to time, 'is the pungent aroma of the spices, the beach with no sand, just pebbles so hot they burned my feet, and the cool of the mosques.' Or she talked about how 'the Gods are a prerequisite for human beings, they're the spiritual dimension of our flesh, and the sad thing is that this fundamental principle has been made out to be something which depends on faith. What a mistake!' she said. 'What a mistake!'

I travelled through their lives and their ideas as if they were mine. I also thought, as César said, that one day the Chinese would wake up and start walking all over the West, overwhelming it. I was also convinced that never mind aeroplanes, we'd never get to the moon. And I also shared Mrs Rosalia's belief that the greatest Western literature of the nineteenth century was written by the Russians and the French.

'The labyrinth of *The Human Condition* is as subtle and complex as life itself,' said César, 'and the depth of Tolstoy is amazing even though he talks from the point of view of a contradictory aristocrat with a bad conscience, or maybe that's why... Dostoyevsky shows us Hell, a necessary face of our selves without which we lack the most disturbing dimension...'

These assertions were so clear, so essential, that with the old people tidy order became meaningless. It was of no importance that Mr Gaspar's ears were covered in crusty scabs, or that Mrs Rosalia stank of stale sweat, or that Edir the giant hadn't cut his toenails in ages... Changing the subject back again, César came to say the same thing: 'Essentiality is a transcendental value. If there are so many peripheral things in the world, if most people get lost in insignificant trivialities, you have to bring in essentiality. Nothing unnecessary, no temptation to avariciousness, nothing either of dogma that fuses us into rigidity; break the frontiers of correctness, go beyond appearances, and out of radical sincerity comes a new society, true in its greatness and its miseries...'

But because people thought they were half nuts, when my mother found out I was going there every Saturday afternoon, I had to tell her they were helping me with my homework and that all three of them knew loads of things, and she more or less went along with it.

'They're weird,' my mother said. 'They haven't got a radio, and it looks like he does all the shopping... I don't know, and her reading all day...'

At home a new period of tension had begun as my father was having problems again because of Uncle Pere. Firstly, Aunt Mercè had gone round to the warehouse to tell him they had to work together again.

'Things aren't going well for Pere at all,' my aunt said, in heels the height of your hand and, as my father put it, painted up like a parrot. When he replied that she shouldn't stick her beak into his business, she pretended not to understand what he was talking about and said as she was leaving, 'I'll tell Pere to come and have a little word with you.'

A couple of days later, my uncle turned up at the warehouse like a soul in torment. He made out he'd just happened to be passing by and said he'd only be a second. He looked as if he'd taken a beating, and my father said neither of them mentioned anything about work.

'He's like the living dead,' said my father, 'But I had nothing to say to him. He can fuck off.'

A week later, my uncle went round to the warehouse again, and then showed up every two or three days. In the evening, at dinner or even later sometimes, my father talked about him, buggering the lot of them and cursing the day they were all born. It hurt him, obviously, to see his brother like this, but he said it was a question of scruples and they could never work together again because Pere would just fuck him up some other way. I couldn't remember what they'd quarrelled over, and from what my mother said neither could she, but the fact was that my father talked of nothing else, and went back to going over and over the same things, and jumping from subject to subject.

'Look at the state of these shoes...' he said, taking one off as we were eating, showing us the hole in the sole that he covered over with a bit of cardboard. 'Not him, though, he's got shoes with rubber soles. That lad's feet won't get cold! But me, mine will, 'cos I'm the poor bastard who has to sort everything out... So what if I work like a fucking dog...'

'Don't get yourself so worked up,' said my mother, and he exploded, 'I'll get as worked up as I like, you hear? So now I can't even shout in my own house! You, eat...' he said to me.

But despite all this, I was calm. The odd afternoon I even bunked off my revision class and secretly went down to the Falangist place to help Jaume bind up a magazine they were making. I went there because at that time of day there was no one around on the streets. Afterwards, I usually went home thinking that on Saturday, after I'd had my lunch, I'd see César, Mr Gaspar, Mrs Rosalia, Edir... They'd tell me new things, I'd discover unknown worlds, I'd take part in fascinating debates... It was the best bit of the week.

Purely by chance, I saw Daniel again that winter. He was still working at the glazier's, and after work and at the weekend, he was still doing whatever he could. One evening my father ran into him on the street, they talked for a while, and then he asked if he wanted to go and work for him. Daniel replied that he'd rather finish his apprenticeship, but if there was ever an urgent job on, he'd help him out, except for Sundays when he spent the mornings with his mother, and the afternoons he liked to keep for himself, and to rest. What my father said was that the lad talked like an old man, had sense, and they agreed that for the moment he'd go round to the warehouse when he could fit it in, and all afternoon on Saturdays. My father had a lot of work, a new delivery had come in that needed sorting, and what's more Aunt Lourdes could do with Daniel's help.

Daniel's going and helping my father made me feel a bit ashamed, because although he was a year or two older than me, I could have done the job too, but my father never asked me. Without ever discussing it, he must have worked out that I had no desire to work at the warehouse, and that the idea of me ending up among the piles of sacks turned my stomach. So he was letting me finish school, but still you couldn't get away from the comments he made which were so hurtful, like at the barber's when he said the world was full of layabouts who never bent their backs, the only way to get rid of idleness was to beat it out of people, it was when you were young that you learned the true worth of effort, and what it took to earn a few pence... Daniel probably wasn't as essential as my father said he was, but seeing as he got on well with the lad, and his father had died in jail, he felt obliged to help him and when he saw him, offered him the chance of work there without a second thought. He realised later he could throw all this about Daniel back in my face...

After all of this I had a strange feeling towards my father. I hated him deeply, but at the same time felt a great tenderness because I could see that afterwards he felt bad he'd said certain things. On the other hand it seemed my mother had been trying to avoid tense situations since she'd been expecting the child. She answered more than ever with ambiguities, changed the subject, pretended it was she who was mistaken so he wouldn't get cross... My father talked a lot about moving house. He'd seen this little house with an upstairs, but said he didn't know what to do, the rent was high... My mother kept quiet. For me, moving out of the area would complicate going to see the old people and César even more, and it would suit me better if we stayed on Escornalbou Street, as they were saying... Actually, I always thought that the idea of moving was because they were afraid of a repeat of my brother's illness, as though the place we lived in was cursed and the arrival of another child would awaken the sleeping evils. Before the pregnancy, my father always said the shack was just great – he always called it 'the shack' – and they'd have to get him out of it feet first... And he added, 'And anyone who doesn't like it can go fuck themselves...'

Naturally all of this was contradictory. What did the desire to buy a rug thick enough for my aunts to sink into have to do with staying in that house? He said he liked it so much, despite its being a 'shack', but it was obvious there wasn't any room for another. At any rate it was clear that all of us were getting anxious about the arrival of the baby. I thought about it sometimes, and I was always frightened of the same thing: that the infant would fall ill, that the fevers and the weeping would return, and death's cold hand would run itself over all of us again... When my mother talked to me about it at the beginning, she said that this time everything would be all right, and just the fact she'd had to underline this was in itself significant. We were afraid, and although everyone tried to hide it in their own way, and sometimes we were able to forget about it, the fact was that the birth caused us great anguish, and so we tried to avoid unnecessary tension and rows.

My father, who didn't believe in God or any of that stuff, promised that if the baby was delivered safely he would take one of those big candles, on foot, up to the church of St Joseph of the Mountain. Later on he said all four of us would go, but after a few days he changed his mind again and said he wanted to go on his own and barefoot. Between one thing and another the days went by and as often as I could I went to César's house on Saturday afternoons, and sitting around the oil lamp, listened to them, spellbound.

'The dead,' said Mrs Rosalia one day, 'watch over us, don't ever doubt that for a minute. It's moronic to think that just because we can't see them they're not there. Of course they're there, all of them. This explains many things that seem to us to be out of the ordinary.'

Mr Gaspar didn't believe in any of this. For him, the dead were dead, and with a wave of his hand he brushed away the smoke of his cigarette and his wife's broodings. But she reiterated with great seriousness that the spiritual world was as real as the visible, or even more so, and existed if for no other reason than we held it within us, inside ourselves, in our memories and our feelings.

'In our memories yes...' answered Mr Gaspar, 'but that's something else.'

'No, it isn't something else. And it's not just a question of appearances either, it's a different reality.'

But he moved his head to say no.

I didn't know what to think, but everything led me to believe that Mrs Rosalia was right. The dead were with us. There was my brother, there was Joanet, there was Daniel's father, and my grandfather... If they all came into my head just like that without even thinking, there had to be a reason for it. They appeared suddenly, they were with me, I could feel them right behind me, I sensed their coldness, but they didn't say anything to me, didn't speak to me. I would have given anything at all to have heard Joanet, or be able to cuddle the boy. I would also have liked to take my grandfather's hand, and say hello to Daniel's father. But they were inaccessible. The dead were dead because they were inaccessible, which didn't mean they weren't with us.

Then César came along with a book by Giovanni Papini and read: 'During one of these naps I began to feel that I was not alone. I did not hear voices or see ghosts, but nevertheless I was absolutely certain that somebody was near my bed, enjoying watching me live. This was not a case of external hallucination. None of this was concrete, material, "real". I was sure someone was with me and thinking about my thoughts. I heard not a whisper, nor saw even a shadow; but I listened to my companions' thoughts and occasionally my soul replied, falteringly, to the unknown souls.

'To begin with, these invisible apparitions occurred only

when I was overcome by the drowsiness of fatigue, but after two years they had become constant, and at any given moment, I always had a companion in my room. The ones who came most frequently were my victims. I felt one after another of them come up to me and look at me, without hate. Each of them told me their story, without speaking, revealing their life to me, especially the sensations that had preceded their deaths. They confessed to me that my taking their life had not been the wrong that those who were left behind believed it to be.

'Some had already been tired and without hope at the time I had murdered them; others admitted that the rest of their lives – "now they knew" – would have been worse than the tranquillity of the cemetery.'

'Precisely!' said Mrs Rosalia. 'That's it exactly!' and while her husband shook his head in disagreement, she sat down wagging a spindly dry finger.

Sometimes, when it was time for me to go home, César came with me, and despite the biting wind, we stopped on the way to talk about his job. I had come to know all the characters. Quim, in charge of maintenance of all the machinery, was the big character because of the women and everything, and then there was the foreman, who from lunchtime onwards drank more than he should have and all afternoon kept losing things and making mistakes. Mr Pàmies was fed up with this, and was constantly yelling at him to come into the office so he could tell him off, but he was such a good person he couldn't get rid of him. Esteve, always perfectly shaved, well-dressed, with an incredible ability to add up extremely long sums... Almost all the girls were really nice and would laugh at the drop of a hat, and what Quim said about them was pretty true, because it got so hot in the factory that even in winter they left a few buttons on their overalls undone and revealed their cleavage... He told me about how you could manage to alter the racket the machines and the girls made just by opening or closing a door. Right at the very heart of the factory, where the spinning jennies were, and next to them the weaving machines, the bedlam was constant. But then when you closed the door to the storeroom, everything settled into a kind of distant accompanying roar. And beyond the stores, in the room where they checked over the garments, and in the supervisor's office, if the other door was closed, you only heard a gentle, very remote murmur. On the far side of this room was another glass wall that gave on to the permanently silent entrance hall, which was where Mr Pàmies's office, the administrative rooms and the front door were. As well as Esteve, there was a blonde long-haired girl called Marta working in the offices...

'You know, it's...' he said to me one day, 'I don't quite know how to put it... In today's world this factory is like a dream. There's no other place quite like it, I swear...' And he recalled the dreadful workshops he'd laboured in, with unpleasant people and foremen who were police grasses.

I liked listening to this because the atmosphere reminded me of my mother's stories of before the war when she worked in a mill, before she met my father. My mother's factory might have been bigger, older and more run down, but there were the same sorts of noises and she also had a good time there. She always said she spent all day singing with a friend of hers, which was what she liked most about it, and they knew lots of *boleros* because they played them on the radio and they soon learned all the words.

One of the Saturdays that César walked home with me I found Daniel sitting at the table eating some cheese. My father seemed pleased that he took a chunk of bread in his hardened thick fingers. Then he raised his dark eyes to look at me, and I saw his thickened lips as he chewed slowly. He was thin and his hair was all over the place.

'You want anything to drink?' asked my father. He said no and thank you. 'Today Daniel has worked like a man,' my father went on, and then he said, 'that's why he looks so damned tired.' And he did look tired and you could see he was uncomfortable, but my father didn't realise and pushed the plate closer. 'Come on, eat up, eat up, man...'

After a while Daniel said he had to go home because his mother was expecting him, and I went with him to the front door.

From that day on Daniel and I saw each other more often. Because he didn't have time during the week, we met up on Sunday afternoons at Pere's Bar, and sometimes went walking around the neighbourhood, or went towards the centre of the city, along the tram route. He wasn't one to talk a lot either, and for the first few days we walked alongside each other without uttering a word. With Joanet, we'd always talked about what was worrying us, and with César I never stopped learning because he'd just as easily point out the characteristics of a somewhat modernist building, as talk of the Spanish migrants who came to build the metro, or the year they installed electric light in the city, where the city walls had been when they started building the *Eixample,* or the fact that Gràcia used to be a separate municipality... Daniel, though, knotted his scarf round his neck and walked along slowly with his hands in his pockets, looking around at everything with an air of indifference which gradually I had to get used to.

In fact I went around with him because my father and mother told me I should see lads of my own age rather than much older people like César, so I spent time with Daniel to avoid trouble. But unlike what happened with other people, who I could get to know from how they looked, with him all I saw was these opaque eyes; eyes which bore no relation to his face, on which his cheeks and brows stood out. He wore a beaten up jacket, never wore a coat, and not once did I see him spend a single farthing. For him it was enough to perceive the changes in the shade of the sky, look at the façades of the buildings, and the people passing by. If I asked him in any detail about the work he did at the glazier's he just said it wasn't too bad there, but he was still getting cuts on his hands. He hadn't heard anything of the other lads. His mother was well. Just one day, talking about when his father was arrested, he went a little bit further. Apparently two plain-clothes policemen had been following him around for some time, and he knew it, because they were asking around at his work and amongst the neighbours without even trying to hide it, which made things difficult for him because everyone was scared. It was still a shock when they knocked on the door that night, pushing aside his mother without a thought when she opened the door. Then, at the police station, there was all the rest. Kicks, punches, threats. One of the times they interrogated him they had him on his knees with his hands tied behind his back. When he lost his balance and fell over, they kicked him and threatened they were going to bring his wife there to the cell and fuck the almighty shit out of her right there in front of him. All this went on for days. They woke him up, asked him things about the communists, beat him brainless, made him stand till he fell down... Finally they took him to prison, sick, and left him to die, making a show of taking him to hospital from time to time.

If it was raining we stayed at Pere's Bar; if the rain caught us out on the street we took cover in a doorway and waited for it to stop, and when we went past a cinema we stopped and looked at the photographs and the posters. In any event, he never complained about the cold, never said anything at all about his job, and often answered me just yes or no. When I told him about something I'd learned from César, Daniel listened to me, but at most he nodded slowly in agreement. He never spoke about my father either, or how he treated him, and he wasn't surprised when I recounted how my grandfather had been shot, and that as a result we had something in common.

'Yes, I know,' he said.

That same day I tried to find something else to talk about and invented a story about Antonio. I told him that Antonio had told me about a place where some really good hookers let you in even if you weren't old enough, but he just replied that he didn't have any money. Another Sunday we went as far as Plaça Catalunya, and sitting on a bench he watched the pigeons pecking feverishly at the ground. Later, going up Passeig de Gràcia, I expressed my surprise at the houses there, and what all the balconies and entrances looked like. He didn't even open his mouth. He walked slowly, looking at me occasionally. In the middle of the afternoon we went past a Falange office and because there was a group of people at the door, Daniel raised his arm to them in salute, and I promptly did the same thing.

'Just go and die, will you...' he murmured a moment later, his eyes full of tears, and then he tried to kick a cat as it passed in front of us.

I talked to César about this lad, admitting that I didn't know what was going on in his head, and César replied that it was difficult to know other people.

'With people, you think one thing and really they're something else...' he said, and then talked about the lady who came to see Edir, and that everyone said she let him touch her thighs for money. 'But Edir hasn't got a penny to his name...' he added.

I didn't understand what he meant, but I felt embarrassed to ask, so I just stuck with the idea that I should keep a closer watch on Daniel's behaviour.

Anyway, that winter's great event was the one about the house. It looked like we were going to live half way up Escornalbou Street, in a little house which didn't leak and according to my father had a ground floor and an upstairs, running water, a bedroom each and a yard at the back with the toilet and a junkroom for all the old rubbish. My mother, who was happy, mentioned that the street was quite steep, and my father then started fucking this and fucking that and yelling that he'd never work her out and he couldn't give a shit whether he lived in one house or any other and he made all these sacrifices for other people and they still shat on him and he'd never come across anyone as evil as my mother and people like her had only been born because you had to have a bit of everything in the world. My mother mumbled she was only saying... But he didn't let her finish and asked her if she thought he was simple and if it wasn't enough for her to stick one fist up his arse she might as well stick both.

'Maybe you want me to drop my trousers and then all those shitheads in your family can come round and spray me with weedkiller!' he screamed.

This went on for a fair few days. When he got home from work he shut himself in the bedroom and didn't speak. He bought himself a loaf of bread and a bit of cheese and ate it hidden away before going to bed. He said nothing to me either, and my mother tried not to irritate him, going to bed late, when he'd already been asleep for a while.

'It'll blow over,' she said one night, softly. 'You'll see, we will go and live in the new house...'

And so it was that when we got up one Sunday morning they'd made up and my father told me to wash because we were going to see the house. He shaved twice and we then went out, on foot because it was close to where we lived, up this street which, as my mother had said, was quite steep.

We went crazy over the house. When my mother went into the kitchen she turned the tap on, and when she saw water coming out without stopping she started sort of hiccuping, on the point of bursting into tears. My father told her not to be an idiot and you couldn't just chuck water away, and he turned the tap off roughly. Downstairs, as well as the kitchen and dining room, there was a built-in cupboard in a corner, the yard with the toilet and this shed which was full of old stuff. Upstairs there were three bedrooms, one big one and two little ones. It was all newly painted, had proper electrical wiring, and the floors were clean. In the yard there was even a wire washing line.

'The baby's going to live like a human being...' said my mother, to which my father replied, 'And what about us? Are we a pile of shit?' But fortunately we were already on our way out and nothing else happened.

On the way back down there was a furniture shop on a corner, and my father told my mother to have a look for what we needed and she replied no no no, we'd sort it all out, there was no need to spend so much...

'Bollocks; I told you to look, didn't I?' and I still remember my mother there with her belly, holding on to the metal grille, trying to choose furniture through the window. 'Forget it, forget it, we'll come back one of these afternoons...' said my father after a short while, because the thing was he got nervous in new situations and didn't know how to act. He always said he'd only been to school until the age of nine, but he knew what he needed to know about life, sometimes adding, without anyone ever trying to fathom why, that he'd still never been up in a hot-air balloon, or had it up the arse, 'Which not everyone can say...' But despite showing off how smart he was, the truth was that he was petrified of getting things wrong and people catching him out. He'd immediately fly off the handle and you felt a violent smack on the back of your head or a hand rewarding you with a vice-like squeeze.

Sometimes my father was happy and that's when he came out with these crass jokes my mother enjoyed so much, like his impression of Frankenstein's monster, or when he swore that one day he'd open the door with his willy... Either way, these antics could easily end in tears, and as we knew despite all the laughter, we could never be rid of what my mother called the sigh of the heart, because it could so easily go from joke to fist smashing on table, like the time it started with him tickling my mother but ended with him suddenly slapping her across the face because she was shrieking too much... César and the old people, who could talk for hours about distant events such as the French Revolution which Mrs Rosalia was always bringing up, could also get into arguments, but they were only raising their voices for the benefit of all the folk who'd been dead for centuries.

'Okay, you say Talleyrand was a totally duplicitous cur,' yelled Mrs Rosalia angrily to her husband, 'but I say his elevated vision of politics was just as necessary as the Revolution itself.'

'And a load of crap, too,' he answered, shortly before he lit his cigarette.

The really curious thing was that they immediately forgot their disagreements and the conversation continued as if nothing had happened. Unlike my father, who could go for days dwelling on the same thing, whether my mother had said whatever, or that some bloke was a bastard from hell... At this point I was beginning to think my father was indestructible. It seemed to me that one way or another everyone was vulnerable. The look in Daniel's eyes was a deep dim fathomless land, where doubts resounded at first, and then the unknown enclosed realm of darkness unfolded. The silence he occupied and the bones that stuck out all over his body also gave him away and made you think that even worse could happen to him. César listened spellbound to his mother, and in spite of all the things he himself said, always ended up talking about what she taught him, this strange inexplicable secret that made it possible for any comment at all from this woman, even the most trivial, to be thought-provoking... Not my father; he was all excluding, and even in the deepest of doubts he expressed extreme violence and so much energy that he was impossible to neutralise. Because he didn't listen and didn't let you speak, you couldn't convince him of anything; because he only reacted to his own emotions, you couldn't get him to fall into the trap of feelings. The only solution was what my mother did: let the crisis pass, let things evaporate, let the storm blow over, let subside the venomous rage that would end up savaging you if you tried to stroke it.... It was sad, obviously, but you had to admit that only previously accepted authorities, such as Uncle Sebastià, had any influence over that man.

So it was then that everything to do with the possibility of moving house turned into purgatory, and many evenings my father and mother argued, he shoving her around the whole time, saying that he wished he'd never mentioned any of this shit about the new house, he was totally fucked off with everything and everyone, he'd had it up to here, couldn't wait to see us all dead, and wanted to stamp on us like rats. My mother was also anxious and tired, and so she kept dropping pots on the floor and breaking them, or she'd twist her ankle and be hobbling about for a few days...

I just thought about Saturday afternoons and being able to go to César's house. It didn't matter whether it had rained that week or not, if it was cold, if my father had brought home a big box of plates and glasses and stuff for the kitchen which my mother said she didn't know where to put... Going to the old people's house was the only thing that interested me. In fact, though, even with them we talked about the move, and it was Mrs Rosalia who first made me see the potential of the little room in the yard of the new house.

'I'm sure no one else'll want it,' she said, 'and then you can use it to read in peace and quiet.'

This comment was enough to awaken in me a bit of a dream, not that I dared tell anyone about it, not even Daniel.

I said to myself that it would be really nice to have this space for me, with some sort of bunk to sleep on, some shelves for the books César lent me as well as any I might be able to buy, and a little table where I could write something or other...

But before all the house business, we had my uncle and father's reconciliation, their decision to start working together again, and as ever the good intentions: we won't go back to quarrelling, we look such idiots, we can help each other out, Mercè was right all along. The first time we returned to eating all together my father and uncle hugged each other, and as they talked and talked they remembered my grandfather, my father's eyes got tearful, he said life was a load of shit, and fuck those miserable bastard military, Francoists, Falangists, police and whoever it was who turned my grandfather in. I don't remember if that was the day, perhaps it was another occasion, when he said he wanted to kill a policeman, and he was crystal clear that even if it was the last thing he ever did he'd have the pleasure of seeing a pig die... I do know that my mother started to tremble then and asked him not to say such things, saying she was scared, and had enough to worry about as it was.

The fear we lived in enveloped everything, going round like some illness, and was alive because it was just as much about what had occurred as what was happening and what might come to pass. And it wasn't only us. Everyone kept their mouths shut, everyone hinted at horrors and injustices that inevitably awoke the worst of feelings. We lived in the uncertainty of which tragedy would unfold, of the suffering that was still on its way... It was an immense and real fear which we felt in the air we breathed and which left us paralysed. My mother, depending on the day, spoke in a clipped, cracked, tremulous voice. I didn't tell anyone, but I knew that was the voice of fear. She looked warily at my father, avoided confrontation and endeavoured not to raise questions of money or any other controversial issues.

That Christmas, because my father and uncle had made up, we all went round on Boxing Day to Aunt Mercè's house for coffee after lunch, and I remember her taking my father by the arm and saying, 'You, you half-wit, come here... Give your brother a kiss...' And just like little children my father and Uncle Pere gave each other a kiss. 'Bugger the pair of you,' went on Aunt Mercè, wiping away the tears.

We were all there, apart from Uncle Sebastià: my cousins, Aunt Carme, Aunt Lourdes, my uncles... Everyone was saying to my mother that she was looking pretty big, and she seemed embarrassed. Aunt Neli and my mother were sitting beside each other, chatting away, and I talked for a bit with my cousins, except for Imma, the oldest one, who'd gone to put on makeup because she was going out with some friends of hers. Aunt Carme was all right, relaxed, having some coffee, sitting next to her sister Lourdes. Uncles Pere and Ramon were talking to my father...

Then, mid afternoon, Mr Robert arrived, the friend of Uncle Esteve who had been in the car with him the night of the accident. Suddenly, as Aunt Mercè sent the maid off to fetch another box of biscuits, Mr Robert started to cry, and said, as though he couldn't breathe, 'I can't... I can't...'

Everyone was stunned; my father went about as white as a cigarette paper, and Aunt Mercè tried to take Mr Robert off to another room, but he said he had to breathe, hadn't got enough air. When he'd completely stopped crying he covered his face with his hands and approached Aunt Carme.

'Carme...' he said, 'I couldn't save him, I swear I couldn't save him...'

Uncle Ramon, who was on good form that day, said that was enough, it was all in the past, the best thing was to forget about it, but Mr Robert seemed totally destroyed and wouldn't be separated from my aunt. He said he couldn't live with this inside him, it woke him in the middle of the night, he remembered it all with great precision every day, he just could not forget every little detail, and he relived time and again the moment when Uncle Esteve, laughing, turned to him with one of his jokes and then suddenly, for no reason at all, he lost control of the vehicle and very slowly, 'Because it all happened very slowly,' he said, the car skidded on the black road, skated as if it was on ice, and as it went, they both knew that it might be serious.

'I don't know if he braked; I suppose he did,' said Mr Robert, and for a moment we all listened as if we couldn't actually remember how my uncle had died and he had to tell us the whole story. 'Esteve hadn't had any more to drink than me, and I was fine, so if he lost control it was because God wanted things to turn out that way. He just turned round, that's all, took his eyes off the road for a moment and nothing more, but I felt a slight jerk and I saw him grabbing at the wheel and I felt we were sliding along this wide road, and it just went on and on...'

'That's enough!' said Uncle Ramon. 'That'll do.'

But Aunt Carme said to let him speak and that the moment when she had lost her man was the most important of her life and she wanted to know how it had all happened and wouldn't be able to rest until Robert had told her everything about it face to face. So she took him by the hands and asked him to continue.

'Don't be afraid,' she told him.

Aunt Mercè had her hand to her mouth, my mother and Aunt Neli looked startled, my father and Aunt Lourdes didn't know which way to look, and Uncle Pere was almost shaking because he couldn't bear hearing about disaster or illness. My cousins and I listened attentively and in silence to this man as he stumbled to tell my Aunt Carme about the accident in which her husband had died.

'I don't remember hearing any noise. It's strange. Just that jolt and this sensation of gliding, and then everything went slowly, so slowly that I could take in the slightest movement Esteve made, the way he turned to look towards me. Then I saw his hands gripping the wheel, as if by holding it tightly he'd be able to make the danger go away. That's when it seemed to me that he moved his foot, as though he was trying to brake, and I felt forced back until my body was thrown towards the glass and luckily I was able to stick my hands out in front of me. But beyond the glass, and the sides of the vehicle, maybe the roof too, we were in thick vegetation, which had grabbed hold of the car like talons scratching at the metal. The slope meant we slid downwards, destroying all the bushes that must have held us up as we fell, but which didn't stop us bursting through at the bottom of it all. Esteve was aware of what I'm talking about too, because when we entered this black space where we seemed to float, free of the bushes, he opened his mouth and I'm sure he said something to me. But I couldn't hear him. Between us there was such a great distance no sound reached me. You know, in a way what was happening to us was beautiful, and if we weren't missing Esteve now, I'd have to be grateful for the suspension of time, the slowing of movement, the lightness we experienced. But Esteve is not here... Because then, I don't know, it all changed. It was as though after flying for an instant we landed on an even steeper slope and started somersaulting down. I felt my legs getting tangled up and there was no way I could undo them, and I could feel each time the roof hit the ground, tearing it apart as if it was made of paper. Then it must have been the impact, but I don't remember it. What I do remember though is having gone through a feeling of silence, and when I took my face away from the glass I turned to my left and said to Esteve that we'd stopped falling. But Esteve was motionless, with the steering column stuck through his chest, asleep, with his eyes closed. That's what I remember.'

Aunt Carme got up very slowly, hugged Mr Robert, and then withdrew to the bedroom, Aunt Mercè rushing to be with her. The others were in tears, especially Aunt Lourdes, who always felt a bit alone. My father said fuck all this bastard bad luck and Uncle Pere looked at him.

''Twas on the Feast of Stephen...' said my mother, and my father immediately leapt to his feet like a wild animal.

'What the fuck are you saying, you idiot! Can't you keep your gob shut?'

She tried to cover up, pretending she was only talking to Aunt Neli. But it was in fact true that 'twas the Feast of Stephen, and later on, as we were leaving, my father was impossible, bad-mouthing everyone, buggering all and sundry and saying he'd kick the fucking shit out of the first person who pissed him off. It had been some time since I'd seen him like this, with his fevered eyes, as though he was on the point

177

of losing control. As he was opening our front door he shoved at my mother, almost knocking her over, and because the door was sticking he gave it a vicious shake until it opened.

He went straight off to bed without a word and once he was in the bedroom my mother twisted her finger into her temple, silently indicating to me that he was off his rocker. Really, there was no way of knowing what was going on with him or why he'd gone like that. Was it because of the story Mr Robert had told? Was it because of what my mother had said? Every time we went to Aunt Mercè's house he came away in a bad temper, just like before when we were going to Aunt Carme's, when exactly the same thing used to happen. So, maybe it was because they lived well and had a decent house, and he felt bad that he couldn't provide the same sort of thing for us. On the other hand all this didn't happen when we went to Uncle Sebastià's house, which was also big and smart. It was only with my aunts that this sort of envy was aroused in him.

That year for Kings' Day, the day of present-giving, my father spent all he had and what he didn't have, according to my mother, on gifts for everyone: for her he bought a new coat, clothes for the new baby, household things to replace worn-out stuff and a heater that didn't smell. For me, he bought a new wallet, gloves and a big box of crayons. Even my cousins each got their own present. When we went round to my auntie's house to give them, it was raining. I remember Uncle Pere saying my father was crazy, he couldn't just chuck money away like that, and my father told him that one of these days he was going to stick a hot poker up his arse. Both my aunt and mother asked them not to have a row on a day like this, and we then stayed for lunch and afterwards the four of them sat down to a game of ludo.

They talked a lot about the new house, if we'd move or not, and the deposit my father had already paid... Aunt Neli, throwing the dice or arranging the counters, kept saying over and over, 'I would...'

My mother kept quiet. That evening, as we were going home, my father said, 'My brother's all right, isn't he?' and my mother replied, 'Yes.'

'If only he wasn't such a moron,' he added.

But then the inevitable happened. Because it just couldn't be that my father suddenly had the money to rent this house, was thinking of buying new furniture, giving my mother new things for the kitchen, having Uncle Pere and Auntie Lourdes working with him, Daniel too, from time to time. It had never occurred to me, but it was as though a blindfold had been taken off and I realised that this warehouse with its asbestos ceiling, miniscule weighing machine and ancient sorting table would struggle to produce all this. My father could tell the difference between wool and cotton, and spent hours and hours going through the offcuts and getting the dust out, but when you thought about it, it was hard to see how this on its own, with the energy he put into it, could be sufficient to feed so many people, and have him boasting around the bar as he did: he could afford to lose whatever it was at cards, maybe he'd move house, his wife didn't want for anything... He always went too far, and in the summertime when we went out for the evening air I myself had heard him with his bluster and bravado about things which were only half true.

'One day it'll all come back to haunt you,' Uncle Pere often told him, but my father responded as he answered everyone: 'It can haunt my fucking arse,' and that was enough for him.

Anyway, one freezing dismal evening he didn't come back

from work. He didn't really have a fixed timetable, but if he wasn't angry he'd generally be home by suppertime, with or without my aunt. After he'd had something to eat he might go out to the bar to play cards, or he might go without eating anything first, but he still came home to wash and change into clean clothes. But that day the hours went by and he didn't return. My mother had laid the table, and she and I waited for him, anxiously not knowing whether on his return he'd say we should have eaten without him, or that he wasn't hungry, or what the fuck were we doing pointlessly wasting electricity at that time of night; and then again, if we were already eating, he'd most probably tell us off for showing no consideration for those who did all the work, in this house no one has any shame, and it was just great for me to make my father eat alone, like some sort of animal.

We waited for him with the radio on, listening out for the sound of the door to the yard to put the supper on the table. At this hour, my mother was tired but she still sat on the edge of her chair ready to get up as soon as he arrived. What I mean is we weren't worried. It was strange he was taking so long, but we weren't alarmed. Suddenly we heard the door and my mother leapt up as if a rocket had been fired up her arse and she went into the kitchen. I turned the radio off and went to my room in case my father was in a bad temper. But it wasn't him, as I quickly discovered on hearing my mother's startled voice.

'What's happened?' Then I saw it was Uncle Sebastià and Uncle Pere. As far as I could remember, Uncle Sebastià had only been to our house when the boy died, so for him to come round meant something really serious was going on.

'Don't be alarmed,' he said, and my mother, with a wooden

spoon in her hand because she'd been stirring the onion soup she'd made, looked first to Uncle Pere and then to Uncle Sebastià, fearing the worst. 'Your husband's been arrested,' said my uncle.

On one occasion at home, I don't remember why, there'd been a dreadful row and my father, after a lot of shouting, smashed the wine jug against the wall, lashed his foot out at the table, and like some lunatic, threatened to slice my mother open and then slash his wrists. I know my mother was crying, frightened, and I was in my room, on my own, feeling warm pee running down my legs. Well, that day the same thing almost happened, but I only wet myself a bit and my mother was at a loss as to what to do, she was so dazed.

And then Uncle Pere started to criticise my father as I'd heard him do so many times before: that all these weird dealings of his would bring us trouble, he didn't want to know anything about this way of doing things, he wasn't going to tell him again... But Uncle Sebastià silenced my uncle with a slight movement, and calmly explained to my mother how it had all happened. My mother, sitting down with the spoon still in her hand, listened without a word. As my uncle spoke, I remember thinking that the way things were going we wouldn't be moving house, I wouldn't get that storeroom in the yard to read in, I'd have to share my room with this new baby, and we'd have to go on fetching buckets of water into the house from the fountain... But my uncle was talking about other things.

As far as I remember, my uncle said that my father was at the police station, there was no news of him, they'd gone to get him at the warehouse in the middle of the afternoon when only Aunt Lourdes had been there. Apparently there were two men in hats, and as soon as my aunt saw them she

181

got the wind up, although all they said was they wanted to speak to the boss.

'In normal circumstances,' said Uncle Sebastià to my mother, 'this wouldn't worry me. There are lots of scams going on, and this would just be another, but there's more to it here. They'll soon find out about the family antecedents, they'll question people, it'll come out that your husband goes around saying undesirable things, such as all this about killing a policeman. We'll see if he's been saying it around that bar where he throws his money away on card games. So for the moment I think we should expect the worst and be aware that besides the stolen goods there are these other matters. Do you understand?' My mother nodded her head and my uncle continued. 'This happened at four o'clock. That they haven't been here yet is a good sign, but you need to tell us where all the papers are, in case there's anything which could be compromising.'

'I don't know,' said my mother, and this was true, because my father hid all his things away so no one would touch them. But seeing as there weren't many places where it could all be, the three of them went into the bedroom and carefully emptied out the wardrobe. Behind the sheets, in a shoebox, they soon found what they were looking for. Uncle Sebastià carried the box through to the table and emptied it. In amongst the invoices, delivery slips, and those sheets of paper with all the adding and subtracting my mother had helped go over, there were two photographs of a naked woman.

'He is an idiot,' Uncle Sebastià mumbled as he looked at the photographs, and then he told Uncle Pere to tear up everything that wasn't a proper invoice and its corresponding delivery note. As Uncle Pere did what he was told, Uncle

Sebastià and my mother continued searching through every corner of the house. They even looked under my bed and on top of the cupboards. They didn't find anything else.

'But what's been going on?' asked my mother later, a little calmer, when they stopped their search. My uncle explained what in fact we already knew: that my father had been getting stolen goods from a factory, in a deal with someone who worked there at night, paying for a thousand kilos but taking four thousand and splitting the proceeds. This had been carrying on for some time, and seemed to be going all right, but in the end and for some reason or other, as always happens, the truth came out.

'After lunch your husband and Pere went to the warehouse,' my uncle continued, 'and it was then that Lourdes told them that these men wanted to talk to him. He got scared and apparently wanted to run, but Pere convinced him to stay, that that was the best thing he could do really. If he had cleared off, he'd really be in the shit, because these police people would have thought there were other things being concealed. Later, when the policemen came back, they confirmed his identity and started asking questions to establish whether he'd bought any stolen items, to which he answered no, completely pale, white as a sheet as always: he earned his living getting waste from the factories, all sorts of rubbish, sorting through it and selling it on; the whole thing was legal. Then the police started shoving him around and grabbed him by his clothing, telling him not to waste their time. They didn't say a word to Pere, thinking he was an employee; then they bundled him roughly into a car and took him away. Then Pere called me and we tried to find out where he was. He's at Via Laietana,' said Sebastià.

'My God...' said my mother as she sat there on a chair, because she knew that at the police stations they used to beat up the prisoners to the point of maiming them, like poor Mr Daniel, but that at Via Laietana they even killed them. That's where they took the ones with political problems, the ones they thought were dangerous, the ones they wanted to really squeeze information out of.

'In any event,' said Uncle Sebastià, 'remember they've only arrested him for buying stolen goods.'

'But seeing as he's a moron and goes around saying things about killing policemen, and other stuff...' said Uncle Pere again.

'What other stuff?' asked Sebastià.

'Oh, what do I know, all sorts: that he's an anarchist like his father, the Falangists are dangerous... When he starts babbling away he doesn't stop, you know what he's like.'

'And who does he say all this to, all these things?' asked Uncle Sebastià, and Pere replied that if he said all this to him he must have been saying it to other people. 'Perhaps that's not quite the way it is,' said Uncle Sebastià, who went on to explain to my mother that he'd telephoned a lawyer friend of his who'd been able to find out where he was. He hadn't been able to speak to him, and they'd just told him that my father was a *dangerous thief*. 'But that's the least of it,' said my uncle, running a very white hand through his thinning hair.

While he was talking to my mother, I couldn't quite believe my father had been arrested. I mean I thought it was strange that someone had made him submit so easily, made him shut his mouth and then locked him up in a cell. If it was true they beat up people they arrested, I wondered what my father would do if they laid a hand on him, he who with us

184

was so brave, always threatening, or saying at the barbers that if anyone so much as raised a hand to his face he'd grab him by the throat and never mind the consequences he'd rip his stupid head off... It wasn't that I wished anything bad on him, for them to hurt him, but I saw in what had happened some kind of lesson of submission and punishment that I thought was just. I would have liked to have been the one who showed him that he couldn't treat people as he treated us, that he couldn't always resolve things by hitting, shoving, shouting and choking. But neither I nor my mother could do anything about the blind power that sometimes overtook him, against the violence that had us cowering. That's why to an extent I thought what was happening was fair. It was fitting that someone should shatter that attitude of being the great know-all, never listening to anyone, believing he could always get what he wanted, being the tough guy, the one who could do anything...

But then, once I'd had these thoughts, I felt tortured by remorse, and it dawned on me sadly that even in such a situation he ended up winning, because somehow it was thinking he deserved to be arrested that was causing me all this distress... And so I found it hard to breathe; I returned to a state of fear, realised my father always won, and that neither I nor my mother could do anything about it...

As my head splashed around all this, Uncle Sebastià ran through a whole series of things we should do. I couldn't hear everything, and didn't catch lots of words, but more or less what he was proposing was that once we'd established that there weren't any compromising documents at home or at the warehouse, the best thing would be if my mother and I went to stay at Uncle Pere's, where we'd be all right until things were sorted out. All this would take time, he'd already spoken to Carme and Mercè, best they didn't get involved, he'd be in touch with the lawyer to find out exactly what the charges were and what could be done about it... But my mother interrupted him to say no. I was surprised how strong her words were, and my uncle didn't need to bother saying any more.

'No,' she said, 'the boy and I are staying here at home. You do whatever you think is best with all the papers, your sisters and the lawyers. I don't know about any of that. But I do know about home, and the boy and I are staying here.'

I was full of admiration for her. As far as I could remember she'd never dared say no to my father about anything, never stood up to him, never put her foot down. Aunt Neli had more than once told my mother about when *she* had got married it was immediately obvious how important it was to make clear to her husband just how far he could go. Their wedding night, because he was hurting her and she complained, apparently Uncle Pere slapped her, and she got dressed and ran out of the house, and it was two weeks before they got back together, with a few things made clearer... She was always telling this story, Aunt Neli. They're all animals; all the brothers and sisters are the same, except for Sebastià because it's not quite the same blood, maybe that's why he's different... But you can't let him raise a hand to you, said Aunt Neli, and my mother replied that if she ever did anything like that she'd be dead already; my father had no consideration at all, and more than once had put his hand to her throat and squeezed hard saying as he did that if he ever caught her lying to him, or fucking around with other men or anything like that... On that day, however, my mother was capable of saying no to Sebastià, who, for sure, nobody had ever contradicted, or disagreed with his plans. And he, who must have realised how determined my mother was, or maybe he was thinking about something else, said all right, do whatever you feel is best, and if you need anything at all give me a ring straight away.

'Yes,' my mother said, and I saw she was breathing more easily and that she couldn't stand the thought of living at my uncle's house and all day talking about the same thing. My father this, my father that, did he say things he shouldn't have, is it all going to end up in some ghastly horror, he's an obstinate shithead, he's got nothing between his ears...

That night I couldn't sleep, and my mother can't have either, but both she and I were absolutely still and silent, fearing a knock on the door bringing us bad news, and enjoying a strange peace. The hours passed slowly. When I thought it ought to be already time for the sun to rise, all I could see was the moon between the two shutters. Then nothing, that never-ending silence... And after many many hours, my mother got up for a moment, put a light on, and I was able to see the alarm clock. It was only one o'clock. After a while again the darkness, the quiet, and all these things dancing around in my head which I couldn't quite put in order. Some moments I could see my father shouting, raising his fist, making faces, then I was at school, blankly going through the day, simply watching to see if the windows got steamed up, or admiring the next boy's effort as his tongue stuck out while he was drawing. Then the globes on the ceiling lit up suddenly and I could see the teacher watching us from the dais. I imagined my father on a bunk, asleep, or on the floor with no mattress or anything to cover himself with, freezing cold, or maybe they'd beaten him and he was unconscious. I saw him in his underpants, as though he was going out to the yard to wash, with his thin legs, his face full of fear. I also saw him up against a wall, his eyes covered, lots of men with guns about to kill him. 'No, can't be,' I told myself, 'can't be,' and I thought if they kill him it's my fault for being glad they arrested him... 'I was unhappy,' I said to the men, 'I just wanted him to see that...' When they fired their rifles, when the shots of the weapons rang out and the smoke emerged from the barrels, my father fell, his knees gave way and he folded, sank, and I was suddenly by him, saw him lying there on the ground, and fearfully took the black cloth off his face to look at his eyes. They were open, lighter than ever, full of fury, accusing me of things I knew I hadn't done... And then, if my father came back, I couldn't work out how he'd react with us after all of this was over. What would he accuse us of? What would we have done wrong? What would we be guilty of? And if he didn't come back, if it all went the way it did with Daniel's father... Then I would have to go to work, I'd have to take care of my mother and the baby, but on an apprentice's wage there's no way we could live so I'd have to go and talk to Uncle Sebastià to find out what to do...

For hours I went through cold, fear, worry, but at times felt a new tranquillity, a feeling of well-being that I couldn't describe and had to do with the certainty that whatever happened, my mother and I, and the baby on the way, would manage to keep ourselves going. If Daniel had done it, I told myself, I could do it too... If I had to work with Uncle Pere in the business, if he ran it, I'd help him, I'd push myself to learn it as quickly as I could, I'd carry on what my father had started, I'd give up reading, give up going to see the old people, wouldn't talk with César, nor with Mrs Rosalia. I wouldn't have time for any of that, I'd have to work like a man... But the baby, what would the baby be like? Would it be like the other one, the one that died on us? It was strange to think about a person you didn't know yet. What colour would its eyes be? Would they be light like my father's?

The next morning my mother and I woke wearily at six when it was still dark. The house was freezing and we dressed ourselves up carefully in our Sunday best. Then we had breakfast and at eight were at Uncle Pere's house. They'd just got up and when they saw us thought there was some news. Later on my mother and uncle went down to the shop to telephone Uncle Sebastià. He didn't know anything, he said; he still hadn't been able to speak to the lawyer. It was too early. We had to telephone later.

Mid-morning we went down again. My uncle wasn't there, but had left word for us to go round to his house before lunch. They would all be there, Aunts Mercè and Carme, Uncle Ramon, Auntie Lourdes, everyone... All I wanted to do was tell Mrs Rosalia, Mr Gaspar and César what had happened and about all the contradictory thoughts that kept coming into my head. I'd tell them about this firm attitude of my mother's, that when we went to Uncle Pere's house she took me by the hand as if that would give us strength... Once, César had told me that his mother didn't love her daughter, and that the whole thing about the armchair she'd taken was just an excuse. She didn't love her and that was that. She herself, Mrs Rosalia, had more than once let slip that the girl was too far from what she considered to be the acceptable minimum. It wasn't that I didn't love my father. That wasn't it, but I would have liked the arrest to have been somehow connected to the fear he'd made us go through... But as soon as this thought came to my mind I was afraid he'd find out about it, that someone or other, by some mysterious means, would tell him that it was me who had brought about his misfortune, as maybe I had brought about Joanet's...

When it was time for the meeting, Uncle Pere suggested that I go and wait with my cousins and Aunt Neli, but my mother again said no, I'd stay with her, I was big and had to know what was going on with my father. Afterwards, on a tram, I realised she was looking at me, and at one point she hugged me gently and said in my ear, 'It'll all be alright.'

And I replied, 'Yes.'

Like all the family meetings, it was chaotic. Aunt Carme didn't go because when she found out what had happened she was in a very bad way. Auntie Lourdes was in a daze, blaming herself for not having warned Sebastià sooner, and perhaps avoiding the arrest. Aunt Mercè, very nervous, kept repeating there wasn't much she could do, her husband didn't know anyone, and it was best for Sebastià to deal with all the things that had to be done. Uncle Pere wanted to know if it was best to keep working or close down the business, and wondered if they could sell the stock they had there or not. In fact, the meeting was only of any use for Sebastià to confirm that my father was incommunicado and that according to the lawyer the inspector had said that for the moment they were investigating *who this individual was*. No one knew how, but the lawyer had found out my father was all right, they hadn't hit him much, and that it wasn't at all clear what he was accused of. It would all be clarified in the next forty-eight hours, but then again it might take longer.

My mother, seated in an armchair, seemed for the first time in her life not to hear a word her brothers and sisters-in-law said. She was pregnant, all she had was me, but despite the lack of sleep that showed on her face, she seemed calm. While the others talked, she waited, and then asked Uncle Sebastià what he thought might happen, the way things were going...

'It all depends what they find... Is there anything hidden away we don't know about?' my uncle asked. And my mother, when she'd thought about it for a while, replied no, she didn't think so.

'My husband just gabbles, you know how it is...' she said, and Aunt Maria fixed her with a glare that condemned her for ever more.

'So we've got to wait...' said my uncle, to which my mother softly agreed. Before any of the others said anything, she got up and said that if it was all right with him she'd continue to telephone. Then she and I left my uncle's house and started walking.

'Do you know the way home on foot?' she asked me after a while, and because I said yes we carried on slowly in silence, wrapping ourselves up as best we could.

An icy wind was blowing, slashing our faces, making us feel as though we had no clothes on. I felt it in my legs, my arms, my chest, my back... That day it did us good to point out specific things beyond ourselves: the biting wind, the cold façades, puddles covered in a thin fragile sheet of ice that you only had to touch with the toe of your shoe to break... The sky was grey, low, extinguished. There were few people on the streets and many bars looked closed and lifeless. From time to time we'd see a black car, or a taxi. A tram rang its bell and went past us noisily as though it was about to fall apart. My mother said she'd never been down these streets, that when she went to Uncle Sebastià's house with my father she'd always gone by tram. We cut through narrow empty alleys, went up broad streets and as we passed the Sagrada Familia my mother wanted to stop for a bit to have a look.

'It's big,' she said. Then she said maybe they'd never finish it... 'Imagine the amount of cash that thing cost...' she added. We went all round the temple, but then the wind got even stronger and we went on walking, up and left, along the straight streets and across the angled corners, until we reached Freser Street. 'Now I think I know where I am,' said my mother after a little. Actually, it didn't take us much longer to arrive home.

When we opened the door the house seemed abandoned, silent, dead, and a knot formed in my throat. Perhaps it hadn't really been till then that I took in what was happening. I knew they'd got my father, knew he was at the police station, but hadn't grasped that that night he wasn't going to be coming home, we might not see him for a long time, and he might end up in prison for stealing a few rags of cloth... He'd done it for us, I was telling myself then, he'd done it because he wanted us to have that bigger, better house... And in my room, in silence so my mother wouldn't notice, I started crying.

Later on, neither she nor I felt like supper, and we just had a bit of fruit. Before I went to bed, my mother told me she was going down to the shop to see if they'd let her call my uncle, and I stayed on my own. Suddenly, into my head came the beginning of that book of César's that I still hadn't read: '*It was about the beginning of September, 1664, that I, among the rest of my neighbours, heard in ordinary discourse that the plague was returned again in Holland...*' I could remember it perfectly, and, according to César, if I started it I wouldn't be able to put it down...

When my mother got back she said there was no news,

everything was the same. Lying on my bed with the blankets round my ears, I started to read. It wasn't clear if the number of dead was normal for the weather they were having, said the book. They were counting up all the burials in the different parishes and implying that some information had been tampered with, but because in those days they didn't have any newspapers and news only spread through letters and rumour... When summer arrived, everything became very complicated: '... for now the weather set in hot, and from the first week in June the infection spread in a dreadful manner, and the bills rose high; the articles of the fever, spotted-fever, and teeth began to swell; for all that could conceal their distempers did it, to prevent their neighbours shunning and refusing to converse with them, and also to prevent authority shutting up their houses; which, though it was not yet practised, yet was threatened, and people were extremely terrified at the thoughts of it.'

The rich people were leaving the city and he, the narrator, after much doubt, decides to stay. He falls ill, is afraid he has the plague, but after three days is better, goes around the city noticing that many houses are abandoned and shut up... Finally sleep got the better of me and I drifted off.

The next day was Saturday, and Uncle Pere came round first thing. My mother feared the worst and called out for me, but my uncle was just bringing my mother the weekly money, and to tell her that according to Sebastià there wouldn't be any news at all through the weekend and she didn't need to telephone him. The lawyer said they'd probably know something on Monday. My uncle also informed my mother that he was going to go on working as if nothing had happened, but had taken down the sign so as to avoid any problems, he said, and that Daniel wouldn't be going to the warehouse for the moment.

'Because of all that with his father...'

My mother thanked him for bringing her the money, and let it out that she was thinking of turning up at the police station to see if they'd allow her to see my father. But according to my uncle, Sebastià had got the lawyer to say that the arrested man's wife was not well, that she was expecting a child and there were some complications, to see if that made them go easy on him... As a result it was inadvisable for us to leave the house. My mother went along with this and responded to my uncle's offers that she didn't need anything, but if it went on a long time we'd see... Later, after my uncle had left, I remember her saying, referring to Aunts Carme and Mercè, that we hadn't had a whiff of the duchesses... Certainly, in this respect my aunts were like my father: they did a lot of talking and got all excited, rattling on about who knows what, but at the moment of truth there was nothing whatsoever.

My mother's eyes were sad as always, but I was surprised how she reacted. That Saturday morning she wanted me to go and help her at the market because she wanted to have some food in. Then she sent me off to buy ice; in addition, before she made lunch, she told me to go and fetch water from the fountain, and she scrubbed the house from top to bottom. As she lifted up the mattresses and pulled out the beds I could see she was tired but determined to do what had to be done. Later we lit the stove and had lunch in silence. At times it felt to me as if my father was dead, we'd never see him again, and that my mother and I would have to get used to this new situation. The two of us living together on our own, with the baby that was on its way, had certain advantages, I told myself, but I was weighed down by a profound feeling of being orphaned, which was liberating and sad at the same time... Moreover, what would happen to Daniel? If he wasn't working at the warehouse, perhaps I wouldn't see him any more on Sunday afternoons. He was a strange lad, and sometimes the thought went through my head that if anything happened to my father, if he was in jail for years, if he stayed there for ever, if he got ill, I might end up like Daniel, thin, shut off, without hope, not wishing to speak... What sense would there be then in going to see the old people? What good would it do me listening to their stories, hearing them talk of books, of characters from the past, of places I didn't even know existed but which became present and real through Mrs Rosalia's words? I would never hear again the story of this Julien, who in *The Red and the Black* almost touches the grandeur of the glittering heights; poor Julien who, with his fascination for Napoleon, rises out of his family's misery, through his own effort, to reach the circles of high society... Finally, carried away by rage, he wounds the woman who was his lover and is condemned to death...

I was also unlucky and also had made mistakes. I thought my mother had wanted to send me to the island and surely it wasn't true. I'd thought that by getting close to Ramon and the gang I wouldn't feel so lonely after the little boy's death, but Ramon had never been interested in me, he was Antonio's friend, perhaps Perico's, at least until he had the operation and lost all interest in working and going out... I'd created a dream that through books I could free myself and find a way out by following the light I sensed at the end of the corridor... But there was nothing I could do. My father's power was infinite, his energy generated an inescapable attraction, everything drew me towards him, and his world was dark and empty like Daniel's eyes.

In the middle of the afternoon my mother got up to go into the kitchen, and on the way she stroked my hair.

'Are you bored?' she asked me. I replied that I wasn't.

Then after a while she told me that if I wanted to go to the house of the old people – she'd always called them that – then I could but not to be too long. I answered that I preferred to stay at home with her, and she replied not to be so saintly, that I should go, that I was dying to... And I went. On the way I thought that on our own my mother and I would get on really well. There wouldn't be any arguments, no shouting, no tension. We both liked listening to music on the radio and the serials they put on in the evenings. Then when I got to the old people's house I found out that Mrs Rosalia, Mr Gaspar and César didn't know anything about my father's arrest. When I explained the facts of the story, she said that the worst tragedies always started like that, with insignificant things, and that you could never get anything at all out of the police. She asked Mr Gaspar to tell the story of the time he was arrested during the dictatorship of Primo de Rivera for publishing an article about the Corporations.

'Things were different then...' he said as if he didn't want to talk, but still he described the two days of interrogation and the atmosphere in the cells...

'Of course things were different then... all this today is more serious,' she said. 'We've suffered a dreadful war, as a result of which this poor man with his family background could unknowingly be one step from prison...'

It seemed to me that Mrs Rosalia was for ever uttering sparkling sonorous percussive sentences, the majority of which were cut down immediately by her husband who tempered them with various considerations. For example, according to Mr Gaspar it was an exaggeration to talk of tragedy, so then she asked him, 'So, are you denying me the right to be graphic?'

'I'm not denying you anything,' he said. 'I'm just saying you're worrying the youngster with your inappropriate comments...'

In fact I was barely listening. It was irrelevant what Mr Gaspar was telling me about what had happened to him all those years ago. My father just wanted to make a bit of money and it was completely different... Moreover, César said nothing; he smiled with his round face, stroking the dog, Sultan, and taking no notice of a cat sitting on the table. I thought it wasn't right for César to admire his mother even when she was wrong. They couldn't take advantage of just any circumstance to make speeches... How come what they'd gone through was more important than our problems? Because they'd read a few books, perhaps? What was so important about books that made them fuller than life? Why didn't they listen to my doubts instead of enlightening me with sentences I could hardly understand?

I suddenly thought they were very weird. Mrs Rosalia and her way of talking was as odd as Edir drooling in the armchair in the hallway. Mr Gaspar was also bizarre, going shopping in the market while his wife read, like my mother said. And César... really I couldn't stand them talking about other things, not realising what that moment represented for me, what might just be at stake... With the excuse that my mother was on her own I left immediately. Once I was in the street I realised I wanted to see Daniel. I wanted to know how he'd felt when it had all happened with his father. I also needed to know if he'd wished, perhaps without meaning to, that it would all be over one way or another. I wanted to tell him that I was tortured by feelings that went from the most profound sadness to an immeasurable desire for liberation. I thought of my father dead, and imagined the life my mother and I and this baby that was soon to arrive would have... This new being that was coming into the house, becoming the centre of everything, colouring my decisions... Without him, everything would be easier, and with time maybe we'd be able to forget what had happened... But then I was crushed by a true feeling of sorrow, and thought over what I could do to save my father, fully prepared to give absolutely anything so he could come back to us...

Daniel wasn't in. There was nobody at his house, not even his mother. I went round to Pere's Bar. Perico was sitting at a table, playing solitaire, with his leg out straight. He saw me, made a gesture with his hand, and kept looking at me. When I was next to him he asked me, checking that nobody else had come into the bar, 'Is it true your old man's fucked?'

I explained to him that he had been accused of buying stolen goods, but that he hadn't known they were stolen when he bought them...

'Oh, right...' he said. 'But he's in a real fix, isn't he?'

'I don't know,' I said. He muttered something.

'Bugger the whole fucking lot of them...' He went on, 'Why don't you go and see Jaume? With all that Falange stuff, maybe they can help you. They're all up each others' arses...'

I didn't know what to do. I stayed with him, waiting for

him to come up with a suggestion that would solve all my problems in one go. Since he didn't say anything, I left the bar. I came to Ramon's parents' shop. He wasn't in either. They didn't know when he'd be back, but he could easily be three or four hours... They'd be closed by then... I also went round to the ironmonger's where Antonio worked. He had a lot to do, had to count God knows how many hundred small parts they'd just bought... He'd heard something about my father being arrested, but the supervisor had been on at him for ages about these bloody parts... I started walking, feeling my heart beating like a drum. I couldn't find anyone, no one could help me, I was alone, completely alone.

'We are born, we live, and we die alone,' I'd heard Mrs Rosalia say one afternoon.

Later on I found myself at the upper part of Escornalbou Street. Half way down on the right was the house my father had wanted to rent. I looked at it from the opposite pavement. The dark door with a knocker, the two windows upstairs with shutters also dark... We'd been down this street so many times with our scooters... Everyone, Ramon, Salvador, Miquel, Jaume, Antonio, Daniel, Joanet... Poor Joanet, I said to myself, forcing myself to think about terrible and sad things; he'd been taken away by a gust of horror and was under the dust... We too, we had all lived and were living under the dust, I told myself, under a heavy dust which crushed us, dirtied us, made us breathe sadness. I loved Joanet, loved my brother, loved my father, didn't want anything to happen to him, wanted him to come back, live with us, not leave us... I wanted everything I'd thought before to be ignored, erased, not to count... 'How many things just slip through my hands,' I thought, without knowing why.

Going down Escornalbou Street I wiped the tears away

from my eyes. I would keep my mother company, be with her, not let her go through anything bad; if my father didn't come back I'd help her unceasingly, work for the baby that was on its way, would never pick up another book again, would drop all this about stories that had nothing to do with anything... Then, opposite the house, I put my handkerchief to my eyes again and went in. When my mother heard the door, she came running out to the yard to tell me joyfully that according to Uncle Pere my father might be out soon... It was like one of those clouts he gave me from time to time and left my head ringing for hours and hours; that and a profound and extremely vivid disappointment.

'Aren't you happy?' my mother asked. And I, dazed, answered her.

'Yes.'

Translated with the
support of
the Ramon Llull Institute

LLLL institut
ramon llull

PARTHIAN

diverse probing
profound urban
epic comic
rural savage
new writing

Independent
Presses
Management

Llyfrau ar-lein
Books on-line

PARTHIAN new writing

parthianbooks.co.uk